A View Of My Own

Books by Elizabeth Hardwick

THE GHOSTLY LOVER

THE SIMPLE TRUTH

A VIEW OF MY OWN: ESSAYS ON LITERATURE AND SOCIETY

SELECTED LETTERS OF WILLIAM JAMES *(editor)*

SEDUCTION AND BETRAYAL: WOMEN AND LITERATURE

SLEEPLESS NIGHTS

Elizabeth Hardwick

A VIEW OF MY OWN
Essays on Literature and Society

THE ECCO PRESS
NEW YORK

First published by The Ecco Press in 1982
18 West 30th Street, New York, N.Y. 10001
Published simultaneously in Canada by
George J. McLeod, Ltd., Toronto
Reprinted by arrangement with Farrar, Straus, & Giroux, Inc.

Printed in the United States of America

Library of Congress Cataloging in Publication Data

Hardwick, Elizabeth.
    A view of my own.

    Reprint. Originally published: New York: Farrar,
Straus, and Cudahy, 1962.
    1. American literature—History and criticism—Ad-
dresses, essays, lectures. 2. English literature—History
and criticism—Addresses, essays, lectures. I. Title.
(PS121.H25 1982)   820'.9   81-9680
ISBN 0-912946-91-1 (pbk.)   AACR2

Acknowledgments

The following articles appeared first in PARTISAN REVIEW:
Anderson, Crane and Millay in their Letters; Memoirs,
Conversations and Diaries; The Life and Death of Caryl
Chessman; George Eliot's Husband; Loveless Love;
America and Dylan Thomas; Riesman Considered; A
Florentine Conference; The Subjection of Women;
Disgust and Disenchantment; Living in Italy.
Mary McCarthy; The Insulted and Injured; and Boston
appeared first in HARPERS; Boston also appeared in ENCOUNTER.
The Neglected Novels of Christina Stead appeared in
THE NEW REPUBLIC; and the review of The Children of
Sanchez appeared in THE NEW YORK TIMES BOOK REVIEW.

To Philip Rahv

Contents

PART THREE | LOCATIONS

Letters

1 / *Anderson, Millay and Crane in Their Letters*

Many people believe letters the most personal and revealing form of communication. In them we expect to find the charmer at his nap, slumped, open-mouthed, profoundly himself without thought for appearances. Yet, this is not quite true. Letters are above all useful as a means of expressing the ideal self; and no other method of communication is quite so good for this purpose. In conversation, those uneasy eyes upon you, those lips ready with an emendation before you have begun to speak, are a powerful deterrent to unreality, even to hope. In art it is not often possible to make direct use of your dreams of tomorrow and your excuses for yesterday.

In letters we can reform without practice, beg without humiliation, snip and shape embarrassing experiences to the measure of our own desires—this is a benevolent form. The ideal self expressed in letters is not a crudely sugary affair except in dreary personalities; in any case the ideal is very much a part of the character, having its twenty-four hours a day to get through, and being no less unique in its combinations than one's fingerprints.

In the letters of artists and public figures we may not find literary charm, but we do invariably get a good notion of how the person saw himself over the years. This vision does not always strike us as "acute"; we are often tempted to put some poor fellow wise on the subject of his own character, to explain that we are a lot more impressed by his dying on the gallows than by his last "God bless you" to his wife. It is difficult to think of a man except as the sum of his remarkable deeds, a statue surrounded by selected objects and symbols. Private letters are disturbing to this belief. What they most often show is that people do not live their biographies.

In the last year or so the correspondence of quite a number of our writers has been published—Pound, Sinclair Lewis, Hart Crane, Gertrude Stein, Sherwood Anderson, Edna Millay—and we have had memoirs on Willa Cather and others. The twenties, which only a few years ago felt so near, are gradually slipping back into that vault called American Literature, where the valuables are kept. The publication of letters is a compliment which suggests the writer is worth a kind of scrutiny not granted every author. As these writers begin to take on that faraway, mysterious, "historical" glaze, publications about them are of considerable importance; a certain ice of opinion, fact and fancy is already spreading over their images. And we cannot assume that eventually all letters, every scrap of interesting material will be published; what is more likely is that the selections, the biography, as we have them now will stand for a time.

It is, then, interesting that the first volume (who knows if there will be another?) of Sinclair Lewis' letters* should be

* *From Main Street to Stockholm.* Harcourt, Brace.

entirely given over to communications he wrote and *received* from his publishers. Indeed, this correspondence is rather good fun, dealing as it does with the finagling, financing and advertising which, though uncommonly exposed to this extent, are in some way a part of literary history, as the billboard is a sort of cousin to the performance. We see Lewis composing a fan letter to be sent by his publishers to all the best writers of his day on the subject of that remarkable book *Main Street;* and wondering if perhaps something special isn't needed for the elegant eye and heart of Edith Wharton. This was all a part of the game, but we may doubt Lewis, much as he liked to appear in print, would have been delighted by this whole volume of business testimony.

Sherwood Anderson's letters* are unhappily selected for quite the opposite reason. They are often bleak and dull to read because they are chosen upon a principle of reckless high-mindedness, a remorseless tracking of Anderson the writer, the artist, the thinker, at the expense of biography. It is felt that Anderson the advertising man, Anderson before forty, was, though alive, a mute statistic; and even after he has been allowed existence at forty only his literary life is permitted. But with Anderson, "the man" is overwhelmingly important. He appears to have been splintered, repressed, uncertain in an exceptional way; in a very real sense his literary equipment began and ended with this painful state of being. Though he could sometimes grow mannered and arty, he is not particularly vivid if you isolate him as "an artist." It is as *a case* that he is unfailingly interesting, this peculiar rising and waning star, this man who brought to literature almost nothing except his own lacerated feelings. This

* *Letters of Sherwood Anderson.* Little, Brown.

latter circumstance, and not his Flaubertian dedication, is what makes us think of him sometimes as a typical American writer. With certain other authors an undeviating, purely literary selection would produce not only the most interesting but the truest portrait of the man: Ezra Pound's life seems to have been, almost literally, an *open book*.

Yet, even if one were to admit the validity of excluding all letters written before Anderson became an author, it seems a bit lofty to omit nearly everything that happened to him during the period of authorship. During these years Anderson divorced three wives and married a fourth; a much-married man without love letters gives us a jolt. There is no letter to Anderson's daughter, only two to his son Bob, who worked with him on the newspaper enterprise; a few more to his son, John, get under the wire because John too is an "artist," a painter, and letters relating to that calling are summoned. This selection makes Anderson seem distinctly hard and unreal; wives are divorced in a footnote or abandoned like unpromising manuscripts, grown children when addressed at all are usually given a lecture on art— and the author himself is as naked as can be, stripped to a man who is writing another book. Anderson's strange, restless soul, remarkable beyond all else for painful, shrinking feelings, is uneasy with his literary friends, Waldo Frank, Van Wyck Brooks, Paul Rosenfeld. Struggling to tell them what he is all about he is sometimes like a tenor with the stage all to himself: "I have been to Nebraska, where the big engines are tearing the hills to pieces; over the low hills runs the promise of corn. You wait, dear Brother! I shall bring God home to the sweaty men in the corn rows." Or again he is not so much complex as hidden and diffuse, singing in a voice not always recognizable from one day to the next. He is a man of the Middle West he tells us, close to the people, and yet all sorts of angels seem to be whispering in his ear, correcting his accent.

Edna Millay's letters*—after reading them you hesitate to know what you thought you knew about this poet. Can this be that sensational young woman of legend who burnt the candle, built the house on sand, kissed so many lips? More than once you find yourself thinking of quite another enduring American type, Jo in *Little Women*, the resourceful, sensitive, devoted girl, bobbing her hair, not to be a flapper, but to pay for Father's illness. These letters are very charming, although not in the sense one would care much to read them if they were not by Edna Millay, or at least by *someone*, for they haven't that sort of power which can be enjoyed apart from a beforehand interest in the writer. They show, for one thing, an intense, unmixed family devotion; not merely an affection for spruced-up memories of colorful relations, long dead ancestors from a region one no longer visits, not earnestness and the urgings of duty, but an immense love for the present, living, impinging kin. This world of nicknames, old jokes, little gifts flying through the mails is startlingly passionate. With friends too there is very often the same extraordinarily intimate style, the same devotion, fidelity, acceptance—and all the while we know Edna Millay was becoming more remote from everyone, enduring very early "a sort of nervous breakdown which interferes a bit with my keeping my promises," and later in hospitals with "an all but life-size nervous breakdown" and at last horribly alone in the country, cold, without even a telephone, dying miserably after a sleepless night. How is it possible with all this fraternal, familial feeling that the frantic, orphaned

* *Letters of Edna St. Vincent Millay*. Harper.

creature of the later years came into being? And how is it possible to begin with that this jolly, loving daughter and sister was in her most famous period in such violent revolt? Edna Millay seems to have had a wretched life, much more so than those persons whose earliest days were marked by a blighting, ambiguous relation to their families and later somewhat toward everyone. There is not anywhere a sadder story than this—the aching existence of this woman who loved and was loved by her family and friends, who, flaming youth and all, married only once and then, to all appearances, wisely. Even Emily Dickinson appears on happier ground in her upstairs bedroom.

It seems likely that Edna Millay's fame and success came too early; the racking strain of keeping up to this is suggested everywhere. And more important: I think Edmund Wilson in his fascinating and moving work on her undervalues the spectacular pain of the sort of success she had. She was a woman famous for her fascinating, unconventional personality, and for rather conventional poems. She was not in the deepest sense "famous" or much cared for by many of the really good poets of her own time. Hart Crane's opinion, written to a friend much stricken with Miss Millay, is interesting: "She really has genius in a limited sense, and is much better than Sara Teasdale, Marguerite Wilkinson, Lady Speyer, etc., to mention a few drops in the bucket of feminine lushness that forms a kind of milky way in the poetic firmament of the time (likewise all times);—indeed I think she is every bit as good as Elizabeth Browning . . . I can only say I do not greatly care for Mme. Browning. . . . With her equipment Edna Millay is bound to succeed to the appreciative applause of a fairly large audience. And for you, who I rather suppose have not gone into this branch of literature with as much enthusiasm as myself, she is a creditable heroine."

This was not an easy situation for Edna Millay to live with. You cannot give, as she did, your whole life to writing without caring horribly, even to the point of despair. And so in 1949 we find that she is planning a satire against T. S. Eliot. In this work she says there is to be, "nothing coarse, obscene, as there sometimes is in the work of Auden and Pound, and nothing so silly as the childish horsing around of Eliot, when he is trying to be funny. He has no sense of humor, and so he is not yet a true Englishman. There is, I think, in these poems of mine against Eliot nothing which could be considered abusive; they are merely murderous."

This is appalling. Edna Millay was not a stupid or even an excessively vain person. She knew, in spite of this wild cry, that the literary approval of Pound was to be valued more highly than that of Frank Crowninshield. (Critics are often wrong, but writers are hardly ever wrong, hide and deny it as they will, in knowing whose opinion really counts.) Her words are not those of a poet secure in her powers, and they are especially harsh for this writer, who was forever generous and warmhearted toward other poets, including nearly all of her feminine rivals. This hopeless, killing bitterness about her own place, as I believe the projected satire reveals, is the end of a whole life which one can at least imagine to have been thrown off its natural, impressive track by a series of seemingly fortunate fatalities. Perhaps she was not meant to go to Greenwich Village at all and certainly not to become famous in her youth. She was sensible, moral, steadfast, a kind of prodigy—among her circle hardly anyone except Edmund Wilson and John Peale Bishop even rose to the second-rate. Not nearly enough was asked of her and she had no time to prepare herself in solitude—until it was too late. It is a tribute, a terrible one, to her possibilities and hopes that she was unable to enjoy the comforts of a strong, public position and split in two. Very few critics can find in Edna Millay's poetry the power and greatness Wilson finds. Still there is something humanly delightful and pleasing in Wilson's obstinacy, like the great Ruskin putting Kate Greenaway among the finest living artists—as he did.

One cannot read even a few of Hart Crane's letters* without feeling the editor, Brom Weber, has made a tremendous contribution. (Of course the "contribution" is Crane's, but he could not have presented his own correspondence.) Fishing about in contemporary literature, Weber has dredged up a masterpiece, for these letters are marvelous, wonderful simply to read, important in what they add to our notion of Crane, and in an unruly, inadvertent fashion quite profound for the picture they give of America itself, and in particular the literary scene from 1916 to 1932, from Hart Crane at seventeen until his death at thirty-three. It is easy with this volume to be reminded of Keats's letters, and if Crane's are not quite so extraordinary as that the same must be said for most of English prose.

Poor Crane—a genius from Cleveland—with his little pair of parents, or his pair of little parents, so squeezing in their anxiety and egotism, so screeching in their divorce, the mother rather beached and given to a humble mysticism, the father, dazed and busy, a business success but not really. Crane's parents are curdling and outrageous by their very multiplicity in America, their typicality; they are as real and to be expected, this young couple, as Cleveland itself. Vast numbers of people under middle age now have par-

---

* *The Letters of Hart Crane*, edited by Brom Weber. Hermitage House.

ents like this and are these persons' only child. Hart Crane was merely a bit in the vanguard by getting there somewhat early. And the son himself, a poet, homosexual, drunkard, a suicide. One had not imagined much could be added to this macabre, but neat, biography. However, what the letters amazingly suggest is the disturbing possibility that Crane had a happy life.

Naturally, he was often much annoyed by his parents, but there is no doubt he was always much fascinated by them. He wrote this middling pair an extremely generous number of lively and often lengthy letters—a source of amazement when we consider Crane's bumming about, drinking, and the dizzy life he had made for himself away from home. In the end he was returning from Mexico, not to New York, but to Chagrin Falls, Ohio, planning fantastically to "be of some help" to his stepmother in the shrunken state of solid assets which became known at his father's death.

Contrary to the guilt feelings usually surmised, Crane seems to have "enjoyed"—no other word occurs to me—his homosexuality, taking about this the most healthy attitude possible under the circumstances. There is not the slightest suggestion in the letters that he worried about his inclinations or was trying to reform; if anything troubles him on this score it is continence, the lack of opportunity. For what it may be worth, we remark that his suicide came at a time when he was involved, and more than a little lukewarmly, with a woman. "You know you're welcome—more than that, my dear, to make this your future headquarters. I miss you *mucho, mucho, mucho!* But I don't think that either of us ought to urge the other into anything but the most spontaneous and mutually liberal arrangements."

Crane also "enjoyed" alcohol—his letters are heathenish in their failure to express intentions to liberate himself from this pleasure. He could, however, be remorseful over his drunken actions and there is no doubt he tried his friends' charity extravagantly. As the Russian proverb about drinking has it, "A man on foot is a poor companion for a man on horseback." Yet Crane somehow never seems to feel he is galloping to destruction. In this he is very different from Fitzgerald, who had in the midst of chaos the rather cross-eyed power of gazing upon his deterioration as if he were not living it but somehow observing his soul and body as one would watch a drop of water slowly drying up in the sun. Crane, on the other hand, expresses over and over the greatest delight in alcohol; he sees himself as a true lover of the grape rather than a snuffling slave of the bottle and, though the results may be the same, the attitude alters the experience along the way. It is one thing to die in ecstasy and another to pass away, moaning, "I knew this stuff would get me in the end." (This is not suggested as the literal deathbed mood of either of these authors, but as a fundamental difference of attitude toward their "difficulties.")

Crane's letters are vivid in every respect—responsive, humorous, beautifully written, fresh—everything and more. The sheer power of mind they reveal is dazzling; his comments upon his reading, his contemporaries, his own work, even the landscape, are always interesting and usually brilliant. It is impossible to think of him, after this, as a natural who knows not what he doeth. What is so appealing about his mind is the utter absence of cant, artiness and fear—all those things Sherwood Anderson seemed to think were the "copy" a literary man was obliged to wring out of his skin. Even when Crane is wounded in his vanity—self-justifying and "true to human nature" as he will be in his explanation of lapses—there is always something solid and shrewd in the way he goes about reclaiming himself. One can see in him certainly a "neurotic need for affection" but there is also astonishing independence and balance. His melancholy is as short as his enjoyment of things is long. Very near the end, before he jumped into the sea, if he *did* jump, he is writing about the glorious Mexican Easter and the wonderful singers in the cafés ("has the old Hawaiian gurgling backed off the map") and detailing his incredibly funny difficulties with a drunken servant, Daniel. "I took the opportunity to talk to him about sobriety—meanwhile pouring him glass after glass of Tenampe. . . ."

Reading these letters it is hard to remember the withered and anesthetized tragedy we thought Crane had become. Yet you cannot easily account for the amount of joy in them and the joy you receive from getting close again to Crane's life. Perhaps it is his magical freedom from true *disgust* that makes you think this "doomed" poet was, after all, under the protection of a charm.

1953

2 / William James: An American Hero

The Jameses were, as Henry phrases it, almost "hotel children." They were packed and unpacked, settled and unsettled, like a band of high livers fleeing creditors—except, of course, they were seeking not fleeing. The children knew a life of sudden change, unexpected challenge, residential insecurity and educational heresy that would nowadays be thought negligent and promising to delinquency. They went from Albany to New York, from America to Europe, from New York to Boston, back and forth, without thought of continuity, without regional roots. Their father was seeking a higher continuity for his children: the old man's restlessness was cosmic and just a bit comic, with his gentle, sweet and outrageous purity of mind and spirit. Yet Henry James says that he would not have exchanged his life at "our hotel" for that of "any small person more privately bred."

It was, no doubt, the very purity of the elder Henry James that gave the family its special nature. The Jameses had tremendous natural gifts for friendship; they were

An introduction to *The Selected Letters of William James.* Farrar, Straus and Cudahy.

talented, popular, respected always and everywhere; they were courteous and eccentric. The father was passionately devoted to his family; he adored being at home and he *was* at home, where he could make out on his considerable inheritance and be privately employed as a writer and thinker. He loved, he doted, he was completely unself-conscious and completely original. Yet the James family was shot through, too, like a piece of Irish tweed, with neurasthenia. Some of it was useful, as perhaps Henry's failure to marry was useful to his prodigious career as a creative writer; some of it was deadly, like Robertson's drinking and Alice's long, baffling invalidism which finally became cancer, providing, as William's letters interestingly reveal, a sort of relief to them all—the relief of an incapacity identified at last.

They were a gregarious family, too. Henry's dinings-out were not more plentiful than William's appearances, lecture dates, travels; Alice had her "circle." The elder Henry James knew everyone in the intellectual world. When William was born, Emerson was taken up to the nursery to bestow a nonsectarian blessing; Thackeray, popping out of the James library, asked, in the way of visitors spying a child of a friend, to see young Henry's "extraordinary jacket."

The James family life, their interior and material circumstances, their common experience have a sort of lost beauty. Their existence is a successful enterprise not easily matched. It is less difficult to understand the painful—Gosse's bleakly evangelical family, Mill's exorbitantly demanding father, or Virginia Woolf's father, Leslie Stephen, who seems to have been nervously exhausting to his daughter—than the special inheritance of the unusually loving. The memorably bitter Victorian family scenes, rich in their merciless peculiarity, are more dramatic and more quickly recoverable than the life Henry and Mary James gave to their children. Henry James writes of his father that "it was a luxury . . . to have all the benefit of his intellectual and spiritual, his religious, his philosophic and his social passion, without ever feeling the pressure of it to our direct irritation and discomfort." Compare this with Charles Francis Adams, in his *Autobiography*, and the *list* of his father's mistakes which he, the son, had never been able "sufficiently to deplore." Adams deplores, and sufficiently too, his father's lack of interest in exercise or sport, he deplores the fact that he wasn't sent to a boarding school, he deplores his parents' failure to think of definite amusements for their children; he ends by announcing, "I do not hesitate to say these mistakes of childhood have gravely prejudiced my entire life."

The Jameses are very much of the nineteenth century in the abundance of their natures, their eccentricity, the long, odd, impractical labors of the father and the steady Victorian application of at least two of the sons. And yet this family group is American, too, and of an unusually contemporary accent: the life at home is relaxed, the education "progressive," the parents, permissive. The elder Henry James was a man of religion, enthusiastically so, but his family did not go to church on a Sunday. They had private means and yet they were utterly unlike "society" people. They might go from New York to Newport to London and back with great, leisurely, upper-class frequency, but they must have done so with a good deal of simplicity and restless shabbiness—they were after all intellectual and magically indifferent to bourgeois considerations. Their style as a family was manly, bookish, absent-minded and odd, rather than correct or tasteful or elegant. They were high-minded but "bred in horror of conscious propriety." Henry certainly later struck many observers as snobbish and outlandishly refined, but at the same time there is his literally mysterious energy and grinding ambition, his devilish application like that of an obsessed prospector during the gold rush. There is a long, flowing cadence in the family tone and an elaborate, fluent expressiveness. Even when Alice and Robertson write, they have an opulent, easy command of style that seems to be a family trait. William sometimes needs to put aside this legacy, as if he felt the Jamesian manner too unpragmatic for this work; but his highest moments are drawn from it rather than from his more robust, lecturing, condensed style.

They were not the "Great James family" until the revival of interest in the novels and personality of Henry James, a revival of the last few decades. Of course, William was immensely celebrated and important, but the half-ironical interest in the elder James, the publication of Alice James's *Journal* in 1934, forty-two years after her death, seem hardly possible without the interest in Henry James. In the effort to understand the novelist, the greatness of the family as a whole somehow took shape. Even the father's Swedenborgianism has been exhaustively examined as a clue to the novelist son. The family mystery, the beasts in the jungle, the "vastations," the obscure hurts have come to have an almost mythical and allegorical meaning. The James family stands now with the Adams family as the loftiest of our native productions.

The life of William James, the eldest child, was filled with energy and accomplishment, but it was not visited by scores of dramatic happenings or by those fateful, tragic events that make some lives seem to go from year to year, from decade to decade, as if they were providing material for a lively biography to be written long after. Actually, an extraordinary biography *was* written: Henry James's *A Small Boy and Others* and *Notes of a Son and Brother*, undertaken as a memorial after William died. Nevertheless, in these surpassingly fascinating works it is always noted that William, the original protagonist, keeps vanishing from the center stage. John Jay Chapman, a friend of William's, says, "And yet it is hard to state what it was in him that gave him either his charm or his power, what it was penetrated and influenced us, what it is that we lack and feel the need of, now that he has so unexpectedly and incredibly died." Ralph Barton Perry in *The Life and Thought of William James* gathered together, with extraordinary industry and power of organization, all the James material in order to write a personal and intellectual biography. Perry uses James's letters, many for the first time, his diaries, his philosophical and psychological writings—everything known about him—and even then James does not quite come through as a character. An equable, successful man is not the ideal subject for portraiture, perhaps, but in the case of William James there is something more: a certain unwillingness to take form, a nature remaining open to suggestion and revision, a temperament of the greatest friendliness and yet finally elusive because of his distaste for dogmatism.

He was born in 1842 and died in 1910. He married and had four children who lived to adulthood and another who died in infancy. "William, perhaps, did not take quite so enthusiastically to parenthood as his own father," says Margaret Knight in her introduction to a Penguin selection of James's writings. *No one* was quite so at ease paternally as the elder Henry James, and yet William's endurance in this respect is notable when compared with that of the usual father. He began, caught up in those repetitions that persist throughout the generations, to cart his children abroad, back

and forth, sending them to this school and that, and although
there are a good many groans and alarms, the burden didn't
seem to waste his energies or thin out his intellectual interests. When he was abroad, he missed the good, old plain
America, and when he was at home, he soon got enough of
the plainness and wanted the beauty of Europe once more.
His family, his writing, his teaching, his lecturing, his
traveling—those are about all you have to build with, biographical twigs and straw of a very commonplace kind. But
no one was less commonplace than William James; his mind
and sensibility were of the greatest charm, vigor and originality. He was not in the least bland or academic as the list
of the pleasant little wrinkles of his nature would seem to
indicate. He is usually thought to be the most significant
thinker America has produced, and everyone who knew
him liked him, and since his death everyone has liked him,
too, because our history has not left a single man, except
perhaps Jefferson, with so much wisdom and so much sheer
delight, such tolerance of the embarrassments of mankind,
such a high degree of personal attractiveness and spiritual
generosity.

Santayana's superb description of James in *Character and
Opinion in the United States* says, "He showed an almost
physical horror of club sentiment and of the stifling atmosphere of all officialdom." And of course we admire him
more and more for that. We commend him with our most
intense feelings for not becoming a mere "professor"; we
note that he did not seem interested in playing the gentleman and that he lived in Boston and Cambridge without its
ever occurring to him that this meant some sort of special
residential gift from the gods. Santayana adds that James
was a "sort of Irishman among the Brahmins, and seemed
hardly imposing enough for a great man." And for that we

thank him, for his escape from dryness and thinness. He is truly a hero: courteous, reasonable, liberal, witty, expressive, a first-rate writer, a profoundly original expression of the American spirit as a thinker, inconceivable in any other country, and yet at home in other countries and cultures as few of us have been.

But James had, as we say now, "his problems." Ralph Barton Perry speaks of the "morbid traits" and the very phrase has an old-fashioned sound of something gangrenous, liverish, perforated with disease. James's "morbidity" is of a reassuring mildness and would not be remarkable at all in the dark lives of some other philosophers. In James, like a speck on the bright, polished surface of a New York State apple, it has considerable fascination, and everyone who writes about the man considers the "depression." It began in his youth, around 1867, and hung on for five or six years. James felt discouraged about the future, he experienced a kind of hopelessness and did not believe that time and change would alter the painful present—sentiments typical of the fixed convictions of a man suffering from a depressive attack. At this time he wrote of his sufferings, *"Pain,* however intense, is light and life, compared to a condition where hibernation would be the ideal of conduct, and where your 'conscience,' in the form of an aspiration towards recovery, rebukes every tendency towards motion, excitement or life as a culpable excess. The deadness of spirit thereby produced 'must be felt to be appreciated.' "

He had somatic symptoms, also—the most striking was the "dorsal insanity," as he named it, the same obscure back pains which had "long made Harry so interesting." He tells a correspondent, "on account of my back I will write but one sheet." The back, for which he went from spa to spa, is an interesting instance of a sort of family affliction in which suggestion seems to play a large part. After James's recovery, the back that had been so much cared for and bathed and warmed and rested was not heard from again. His other symptoms were insomnia, weakness, digestive disorders and eyestrain—the latter the only one usually considered to have had a physical basis.

During the two years in Germany William James felt quite lonely, homesick, and much thrown back upon himself. He wrote his beautifully expressive early letters to his friends and family, letters of considerable length and great energy of feeling and observation. He speaks, in suitably stoical, manly terms of his own illness, but he also speaks of other people, shows a much truer interest in the world about him than one would expect from a man in a deep depression. His suffering is genuine, but it does not override the claims of the impersonal. A common-sense melody sings through the saddest part of the story, although some of this may be bravado or pride. It is hard to know how to estimate the depth of this early collapse.

There is no doubt that occupational uncertainty was the cause of James's low spirits. It is the usual thing of a young man in medicine or law who does not want to be in medicine or law. (Those innumerable poets who found themselves enrolled for the clergy!) Listlessness came on like a weakening fever as the absence of genuine interest became more and more obvious. "It is totally impossible for me to study now in any way, and I have at last succeeded in *genuinely* giving up the attempt to." James puts every obstacle in the way of the successful practice of medicine; there are even moral objections and he does not fail to notice the toadying young medical students must go in for with their professors, the kind of anxious flattery and unctuous activity necessary to advance professional interests. James did not want to be a doctor and yet it would have been difficult for a young man in his twenties to decide that he was going to be a "psychologist" or a "philosopher." One became a philosopher as a culmination, as one became wise or great or full of special insight. In youth it was different, and even the novelist, Henry James, somehow incredibly found himself briefly enrolled at the Harvard Law School.

Moderate and finally benign the depression proved to be, but James *did* have it and other similar emotional disturbances, nightmarish times, and sensations approaching a state of hallucination. His special awareness of merging states of mind, of the blurred flow of consciousness, the involuntary, subconscious mental life was probably sired by the odd helplessness he experienced during his youthful struggles. The case of "The Sick Soul" in *The Varieties of Religious Experience*, an extraordinarily vivid piece of composition, has been widely called upon to give testimony to James's profound experience of the darkest corners of horror. In this dreadful vignette, attributed in the book to a Frenchman but later acknowledged by James to have come from his own experience, he tells of sitting alone in a "state of philosophic pessimism," and of then going suddenly into his dark dressing room and finding his mind involuntarily assaulted by the memory of a poor epileptic he had seen in an asylum. The remembered person was a "black-haired youth with greenish skin, entirely idiotic. . . . He sat there like a sort of sculptured Egyptian cat or Peruvian mummy, moving nothing but his black eyes and looking absolutely nonhuman. This image and my fear entered into a species of combination with each other. *That shape am I*, I felt, potentially. Nothing that I possess can defend me from that fate, if the hour for it should strike for me as it struck for him." This classical experience of abysmal fear, of the dreaded double, of the annihilation of the self is written with a touch of Poe and even of Henry James. The "pit of insecurity" remained long afterward, and James said the whole thing "made me sympathetic with the morbid feelings of others."

James was thirty-six years old when he married, forty-eight years old when his first important work, *The Principles of Psychology*, was completed. For all his energy and genius, there was a sort of hanging back about him, a failure of decision beginning from those first early days of anxiety about his career. He seems to have been capable of any amount of activity, but his ambition was not of the greediest sort. Inspiration and verve made it fairly easy for him to accomplish what he wished, but it was probably procrastination, in all its joy and sorrow, that made him such a great writer on the quirks of human nature. He was a sort of poet of "habit" and "will" and never able to bring himself under their pure, efficient control. A recurring hesitation to commit himself was at the very heart of his philosophical and personal nature. Santayana believed James would have been uncomfortable in the face of any decided question. "He would still have hoped that something might turn up on the other side, and that just as the scientific hangman was about to dispatch the poor convicted prisoner, an unexpected witness would ride up in hot haste, and prove him innocent." This everlasting question mark is part of James's appeal for the contemporary mind. He dreaded Germanic system-making, he feared losing touch with the personal, the subjective, the feelings of real human beings more than he feared being logically or systematically faulty. Everyone complained of the looseness of his thought. Chapman: "His mind is never quite in focus." Ralph Barton Perry speaks of

James's "temperamental repugnance to the processes of exact thought." And everyone realized that it was the same openness that saved James from pedantry and egotism.

Religion: sometimes an embarrassment to James's reasonable admirers. His nuts and cranks, his mediums and table-tappers, his faith healers and receivers of communications from the dead—all are greeted by James with the purest, melting latitudinarianism, a nearly disreputable amiability, a broadness of tolerance and fascination like that of a priest at a jam session. James's pragmatism, his pluralism, his radical empiricism have been the subject of a large amount of study and comment. Reworking the sod from whence so many crops have come in their season seems profitless for the enjoyment of James's letters, letters that are nearly always personal, informal, nontechnical and rather different in this way from, for instance, Santayana's recently published correspondence in which philosophy keeps cropping up everywhere. Religion, on the other hand, was a sort of addiction for James, and all of his personality is caught up in it, his unique ambivalence, his longing, as Oliver Wendell Holmes says, "for a chasm from which might appear a phenomenon without phenomenal antecedents."

Whenever someone near to him died, James could not restrain a longing for the comforts of immortality. To Charles Eliot Norton, when he was very ill in 1908, James wrote, "I am as convinced as I can be of anything that this experience of ours is only a part of the experience that is, and with which it has something to do; but *what* or *where* the other parts are, I cannot guess. It only enables one to say 'behind the veil, behind the veil!' . . ." When his sister Alice's death was obviously near, an extraordinary letter to her said, "When that which is *you* passes out of the body, I am sure that there will be an explosion of liberated force and life till then eclipsed and kept down. I can hardly imagine *your* transition without a great oscillation of both 'worlds' as they regain their new equilibrium after the change! Everyone will feel the shock, but you yourself will be more surprised than anybody else." A memorial address for his old friend, Francis Boott, ends, "Good-by, then, old friend. We shall nevermore meet the upright figure, the blue eye, the hearty laugh, upon these Cambridge streets. But in that wider world of being of which this little Cambridge world of ours forms so infinitesimal a part, we may be sure that all our spirits and their missions here will continue in some way to be represented, and that ancient human loves will never lose their own."

Immortality was a great temptation and so, also, was the tranquillity James had observed to be at least sometimes a result of religious belief. "The transition from tenseness, self-responsibility, and worry, to equanimity, receptivity, and peace . . . This abandonment of self-responsibility seems to be the fundamental act in specifically religious as distinguished from moral practice." James had at hand any amount of sympathy for the believer, along with the most sophisticated knowledge of the way in which the religious experience could be treated as a neurotic symptom by the nonbeliever. At the beginning of *The Varieties* he writes, "A more fully developed example of the same kind of reasoning is the fashion, quite common nowadays among certain writers, of criticizing religious emotions by showing a connection between them and the sexual life. . . . Medical materialism finishes up Saint Paul by calling his vision on the road to Damascus a discharging lesion of the occipital cortex, he being an epileptic."

Some of the enchantment of *The Varieties* comes from its

being a kind of race with James running on both teams—here he is the cleverest skeptic and there the wildest man in a state of religious enthusiasm. He can call St. Theresa a "shrew," and say that the "bustle" of her style proves it, and yet he can appreciate the appeal the Roman Catholic Church will often have for people of an intellectual and artistic nature. And beyond conventional religion, beyond God and immortality and belief, there is the "subliminal door," that hospitable opening through which he admits his living items of "psychical research." True his passion was instructive, scholarly and perhaps psychological in many cases, but that does not explain the stirring appeal for him in the very vulgarity of the cults, the dinginess of the séances. The Boston medium Mrs. Piper sometimes bored him; even his colleague Myers, a much more devoted psychical researcher, called this lady, "that insipid Prophetess, that tiresome channel of communication between the human and the divine." But in the end, James finally said about Mrs. Piper: "In the trances of this medium, I cannot resist the conviction that knowledge appears which she has never gained by the ordinary waking use of her eyes and ears and wits." Even as late as 1893 James had eighteen sessions with a "mind-curer" and found his sleep wonderfully restored. He says, by way of testimonial to her remarkable powers, "I would like to get this woman into a lunatic asylum for two months, and have every case of chronic delusional insanity in the house tried by her."

In 1884, the American Chapter of the Society for Psychical Research was founded. James became a member and was still a member at the time of his death. Working in psychic research was not just a bit of occasional dashing about to séances and mind readings. The whole movement was filled with bickering intensity, with all the nervous, absorbing factional struggles "minority" beliefs and practices usually develop. An endless amount of work went into this research: the communications from beyond tended to be lengthy. In 1908, James wrote Flournoy, "I have just read Miss Johnson's report on the S.P.R. Proceedings, and a good bit of the proofs of Piddington's on cross-correspondence between Mrs. Piper, Mrs. Verrall, and Mrs. Holland, which is to appear in the next number. You will be much interested, if you can gather the philosophical energy to go through with such an amount of tiresome detail. It seems to me that these reports open a new chapter in the history of automatism; and Piddington's and Johnson's ability is of the highest order." On his defense of faith healers when they were being attacked as charlatans by the medical profession, James wrote a friend, "If you think I *enjoy* this sort of thing you are mistaken."

James's son, Henry, the first editor of his letters, believed that it was only in the interest of pure research that his father gave so much time to these psychic manifestations and "not because he was in the least impressed by the lucubrations of the kind of mind" that provided such material. Ralph Barton Perry attributes the time spent to James's psychological interest in unusual cases and also to his natural liberal tendency to prefer the lowly—spiritualism, faith healing and the like—rather than the orthodox and accepted. The picturesqueness, the dishonesty even, seems to have given James the sort of delight that amounted almost to credulity. He would be fatigued and morally discouraged with such people as the Neapolitan medium, Eusapia Paladina, about whom he said, "Everyone agrees that she cheats in the most barefaced manner whenever she gets an opportunity," and yet he concludes optimistically that "her credit has steadily risen." He reports that in England the two daughters of a clergyman named Creery whose feats of thought-transference had much impressed certain strict investigators were later found to be signaling each other. There were many disheartening moments and infidelities. James and his fellow researcher, Hodgson, went on a trip and spent "the most hideously inept psychical night, in Charleston, over a much-praised female medium who fraudulently played on the guitar. A plague take all white-livered, anaemic, flaccid, weak-voiced Yankee frauds! Give me a full-blooded red-lipped villain like dear old D.—when shall I look upon her like again?" In the letters of a few weeks previously he had described the medium, dear old D., as a "type for Alexander Dumas, obese, wicked, jolly, intellectual, with no end of go and animal spirits . . . that woman is one with whom one would fall wildly in love, if in love at all—she is such a fat, *fat* old villain." You do not find the delight, the hospitality, the enjoyment in the other psychic researchers—only credulity and reports and statistics on "controls," those spirits who give off conversation and information to the strange vessels capable of hearing them. One control accused the psychologist Stanley Hall of having murdered his wife.

James seems to have enjoyed all this as another learned man might enjoy burlesque, but at the same time he took it with a great deal of seriousness. His yea is followed by his nay, as is usual with him, and yet he hoped that these manifestations would be scientifically validated, that the endless, wearisome, fantastic proceedings of the Society for Psychical Research would be an important contribution to knowledge. In all this James is a sort of Californian; he loves the new and unhistorical and cannot resist the shadiest of claims. He, himself, and most of the people who write piously about him felt that he died without saying all he might have said, without finishing his system, without in some grand conclusion becoming the great philosophical thinker that he was, or at least without in the end truly and thoroughly writing his final thoughts on the universe and life. Perhaps there is a sense in which this may have been the case, but perhaps it is only the usual scholarly appetite for the weighty and lengthy. William James without his gaiety, his spooks, his nuts and frauds, his credulity and his incongruous longings for something more than life, even though he was committed to testing every belief *by* life, would not be the captivating and splendid spirit he is. It is usual to remember his wit, his courtesy, his geniality, his liberalism, but in the end his image is indefinable and one does not know how to name the quality that shines in every bit of his writing, in all we know about him, in the character and spirit we believe him to have been. Perhaps it is his responsiveness, his unexpected sympathies, even his gulli-bility. Or his goodness. Whatever it may have been, we feel it as something simple many others might have and yet hardly anyone seems to possess. A certain flatness and repeti-tiveness appear in people's attempts to define him, for he is odd but not dark, rich not in peculiarities but rather peculiar in the abundance of his endowment with the qualities and dispositions we admire in all men.

About his letters the same ideas come to mind—were we better, more gifted, more abounding in our feelings we might have written them ourselves. James's correspondence is spontaneous and casual. Letters are not necessarily of that order; every sort of letter, the formal, the affected, the merest scribble or a showpiece composed with all the de-liberation of a sonnet, all these have been at some time written wonderfully by someone. Yet a special regard is given to the impulsive, free letter because such unrevised and personal moments have an authenticity utterly innocent of posthumous longings. They are the nearest things we have to the lost conversations of memorable persons. James's letters are felicitous, easy, genuine as talk, hurriedly written, each for its own occasion, and yet very much written, with all the sense of form and beauty and the natural power to interest that come from a man with a pure gift for the art of letter writing. They are intimate and personal; they have a romantic fullness of emotion; they are the productions of a social creature, a man of the world, at least in the sense of complicated obligations and a conscientious regard for friendships. They have a poetical sweetness; they delight and charm, and they are deeply affecting, even somewhat sad, as they reveal year by year a life and sensibility of great force and great virtue.

It certainly did not occur to William James at the beginning of his career that he was going to be an important writer, that this, rather than painting, was the art he was going to master. Indeed, after his first review he said, "I feel that a living is hardly worth being gained at this price." He spoke of "sweating fearfully for three days, erasing, tearing my hair, copying, recopying, etc." It was often hard for him to settle down to philosophical and professional writing; yet once started, his marvelous clarity, humor, and his superb prose style carried him along rapidly enough. Letter writing, on the other hand, was a pure pleasure, a duty and an indulgence at the same time. His desire, in letters to friends, was to give happiness—compare this with D. H. Lawrence who seemed when he felt the desire to communicate with his friends to want, at best, to instruct, and, at the worst, to chastise. James's affections appear to be without limits. "Darling Belle-Mère," he addresses his mother-in-law and signs off with "oceans of love from your affectionate son." His colleagues are greeted with "Glorious old Palmer" and "Beloved Royce." James is, as his letters show, quite susceptible to women; he is their correspondent on suitable occasions with great and convincing gallantry. He has such pleasure in his friends that the reader of his letters longs to know the recipients—a condition far from being the usual one with great letter writers. (Madame de Sévigné's daughter is one of the last persons we would want to recall from the shades.) Grace Norton, Fannie Morse, Thomas Ward, Henry Bowditch, and Mrs. Whitman seem persons of the most pleasing dimensions as we meet them in James's correspondence. His attitude toward them all is benevolent, loving, loyal and completely without pompousness or self-importance. James was almost *curiously* modest. People crowded to his lectures, he was truly a public figure, and an international celebrity, too, but there is never anything of rigidity or conceit in his character. He hardly seemed to believe he had done anything unusual. His tenderness, too, was of the most luxuriant variety and stayed with him forever. John Jay Chapman thought he always liked everything and everyone too well.

1960

3 / Mary McCarthy

Mary McCarthy! "*The Man in the Brooks Brothers Shirt!*
That's my Bible!" I once heard a young woman exclaim. No
doubt the famous short story is rightly understood as a sort
of parable representing many a young girl's transgressions,
even if it does not concern itself with the steps in the
sinner's rehabilitation. It would be hard to think of any
writer in America more interesting and unusual than Mary
McCarthy. Obviously she wants to be noticed, indeed to be
spectacular; and she works toward that end with what one
can only call a sort of trance-like seriousness. There is something puritanical and perplexing in her lack of relaxation,
her utter refusal to give an inch of the ground of her own
opinion. She *cannot conform*, cannot often like what even
her peers like. She is a very odd woman, and perhaps oddest
of all in this stirring sense of the importance of her own
intellectual formulations. Very few women writers can
resist the temptation of feminine sensibility; it is there to be
used, as a crutch, and the reliance upon it is expected and
generally admired. Mary McCarthy's work, from the first
brilliant *The Company She Keeps* down to her latest
collection of essays, *On the Contrary: Articles of Belief*

1946–1961, is not like that of anyone else and certainly not like that of other women. We might naturally wonder from what blending of bravura and commonsense this tart effervescence has come.

In America we have had the quiet, isolated genius of Emily Dickinson, on the one hand, and that of Edith Wharton, dignified, worldly, astute, on the other, each holding a prime spiritual location in the national landscape. In the background we might imagine the highly usual romantic glamor of Edna St. Vincent Millay, the romance of lyrics and lovers and tragic endings. Mary McCarthy, because of the radical turn of her mind, has little connection with any of these figures even if there are occasional correspondences to Edith Wharton and Edna Millay. And yet how difficult it is to define the image of this writer. If it is popular fame to figure somehow in the scheme of persons who have not had the time to examine the actual claims of the famous person, then she has popular fame as well as genuine literary distinction. Perhaps to the world her image is composed of the clear eyes of the Cecil Beaton photographs, the strong profile, the steady gaze; and it is certainly made of the candor about Sex in her novels and stories and the "attacks" on gods like Tennessee Williams. This is all very unexpected. There is charm and vigor and an almost violent holding of special opinions. She is, as someone said of Thackeray, "an uncomfortable writer."

Not so long ago, Brooks Atkinson, the retired dean of American drama critics, had the sobering occasion to report that Mary McCarthy had been very hard, in a review in an English newspaper, on the bright young English drama critic, Kenneth Tynan, whom she found neither very bright nor very young in his literary spirit and style. The event was dismaying. Where are you if Walter Kerr lights into

Howard Taubman, an unimaginable act of disloyalty for either of those members of the Establishment?

If there were any real ancestor among American women for Mary McCarthy it might be Margaret Fuller. How easy it is to imagine the living writer as a visitor at Brook Farm, a friend of Mazzini's, a journalist in Rome during the 1840's. Both women have will power, confidence and a subversive soul sustained by exceptional energy. A career of candor and dissent is not an easy one for a woman; the license is jarring and the dare often forbidding. Such a person needs more than confidence and indignation. A great measure of personal attractiveness and a high degree of romantic singularity are necessary to step free of the mundane, the governessy, the threat of earnestness and dryness. Moderating influences are essential. Madame de Staël, vexing and far-out as she was, needed her rather embarrassing love affairs to smooth over, like a cosmetic cream, the shrewd image. With Mary McCarthy the purity of style and the liniment of her wit, her gay summoning of the funny facts of everyday life, soften the scandal of the action or the courage of the opinion.

In the novels and stories, the "shocking" frankness of the sexual scenes is very different from the hot prose of male writers. These love scenes are profoundly feminine, even though other women writers do not seem to want to take advantage of this same possibility. In her fiction, shame and curiosity are nearly always found together and in the same strange union we find self-condemnation and the determined pursuit of experience; introspective irony and flat, daring action. In the paperback edition of *The Company She Keeps* we see on the cover a pretty girl posed for the seduction scene on the train—bare shoulders, whisky bottle, and a reflecting pout on her lips. But the picture cannot give any idea of the unexpected contents of the mind of the actual fictional heroine. The psychological fastidiousness and above all the belligerent mood of the surrendering girl are the essence of the story. The sexual affair with the second-rate "man in the Brooks Brothers shirt" is for the heroine both humbling and enthralling; and so, also in the same way, is the outrageous coupling on the couch in *A Charmed Life* of the remarried young wife and her former husband. The heroine, in these encounters, feels a sense of piercing degradation, but it does not destroy her mind's freedom to speculate; her rather baffling surrenders do not vanquish her sense of her conqueror's weaknesses and absurdities. Of course, these works are comedies; and it is part of Mary McCarthy's originality to have written, from the woman's point of view, the comedy of Sex. The coarse actions are described with an elaborate *verismo* of detail. (The safety pin holding up the underwear in the train scene; in *A Charmed Life* "A string of beads she was wearing broke and clattered to the floor. 'Sorry,' he muttered as he dove for her left breast." The "left" notation is a curiosity, a kind of stage direction, inviting us to project ourselves dramatically into an actual scene.)

Plot and dramatic sense are weak in Mary McCarthy's fiction. Taste and accuracy are sometimes substitutions. What people eat, wear, and read are of enormous importance. The reader follows the parade of tastes and preferences with a good deal of honest excitement and suspense, wondering if he can guess the morals of the kind of person who would cover a meat loaf with Campbell's tomato soup. He participates in a mysterious drama of consumption, in which goods are the keys to salvation. Taste is also used as the surest indication of character. "There were pieces of sculpture by Archipenko and Harold Cash, and the head of

a beautiful Egyptian Queen, Neferteete." Accuracy, unusual situations documented with extreme care, mean for the
reader a special sort of recognition. The story "Dottie Makes
an Honest Woman of Herself" is about contraception in the
way, for instance, Frank Norris's *The Octopus* is about
wheat. "Dottie did not mind the pelvic examination or the
fitting. Her bad moment came when she was learning how
to insert the pessary herself. Though she was usually good
with her hands and well-coordinated . . . As she was trying
to fold the pessary, the slippery thing, all covered with jelly,
jumped out of her grasp and shot across the room and hit
the sterilizer. Dottie could have died." This story, *memorable* to put it mildly, could not have been written by anyone
except Mary McCarthy. Reading it over again, the suggestion came involuntarily to mind that perhaps it was
meant as a parody of the excesses of naturalistic fiction, a
parody, too, of the brute, prosaic sexual details in, for
instance, a writer like John O'Hara. There is an air of im-
parting information—like whaling in Melville or, more
accurately, the examination of dope addiction in Gelber's
play, *The Connection*. This aspect of *information* brings to
memory the later story by Philip Roth in which a college
girl suggests she knows all about contraception because she
has read Mary McCarthy.

In a writer of this kind there is an urgent sense of the uses
to which a vivid personal nature may be put by a writer's
literary talent. There is very often an easily recognized
element of autobiography and it is in autobiography that
Mary McCarthy excels—that is, of course, if one uses the
word in its loosest and largest sense. *The Company She
Keeps* and *Memories of a Catholic Girlhood* are richer, more
beautiful, and aesthetically more satisfying than, say, *A
Charmed Life* or *The Groves of Academe*. The condition

that made *The Oasis* somewhat stillborn was that it was more biography than autobiography. In autobiography, self-exposure and self-justification are the same thing. It is this contradiction that gives the form its dramatic tension. To take a very extreme case, it is only natural that critics who find importance in the writings of the Marquis de Sade will feel that the man himself is not without certain claims on our sympathy and acceptance. In Mary McCarthy's case, the daring of the self-assertion, the brashness of the correcting tendency (think of the titles *Cast a Cold Eye* and *On the Contrary*) fill us with a nervous admiration and even with the thrill of the exploit. Literature, in her practice, has the elation of an adventure—and of course that elation mitigates and makes aesthetically acceptable to our senses the strictness of her judgments.

She is not moved by reputation. Indeed her congenital skepticism bears down hardest on the most flattered. Only occasionally, as in her essay on the fashion magazines, does she write about what is known as "popular culture." She does not bother to discuss television, but she might discuss the imperfections of, for instance, J. D. Salinger. In her dramatic criticism, collected in *Sights and Spectacles*, there are times—I think of her remarks on Shaw and Ibsen—when she seems in an uneasy relationship with the great men. Shaw's mad reasonableness is put to the test of her own reasonableness; the toils of Ibsen appear to come off less prosperously than her own toils to define them. One sometimes has the feeling of a mistake in tone, rather than a perversity of judgment, as if the meeting of the author and the subject that everyone expected to go so well had unaccountably gotten off to a bad start.

In her new book, *On the Contrary*, she has written her two best essays: "Characters in Fiction" and "Fact in Fiction." In their manner and feeling these essays suggest a new gravity and sympathy, a subtle change in the air, a change already felt in her large books on Florence and Venice. As for the ideas in the two essays: they are the only new things said about the art of the novel in many years. Paraphrase is difficult because the examples are very fresh and the insights rather angular.

On "Fact in Fiction": fact, "this love of truth, ordinary, common truth recognizable to everyone, is the ruling passion of the novel. Putting two and two together, then, it would seem that the novel, with its common sense, is of all forms the least adapted to encompass the modern world, whose leading characteristic is irreality."

As for "Character in Fiction," the decline in the ability to create character comes, in this view, from the modern tendency to try to reach character from the inside. The author has become a sort of ventriloquist; he is not content to describe but must try to impersonate the very soul of someone quite different from himself. The reader is perplexed; he feels the strain, the insecurity. Water has been put into the whisky; the dilution is the poor author himself, struggling to blend in.

1961

4 / The Neglected Novels of Christina Stead

It is annoying to be asked to discover a book that is neither old nor new. When it must be admitted that the work lacks, on the one hand, the assurance of age and, on the other, a current and pressing fame, our resistance grows and our boredom swells. We feel certain we don't want to read a book no one else is reading or has read. The work being offered to us appears cold and flat, like a dish passed around for a tardy second helping. It is gratifying to our dignity to be able to turn down the offer.

There are many roads to neglect—simple neglect itself, early and late, is far from being the only way. Very often we find that a writer has produced a number of books that were, on publication, well and even enthusiastically received and yet somehow the years passed and the reputation, the fame, the consideration did not quite take hold. The public mind, friendly enough at first, turned out to have been but briefly attracted; the literary mind was, at the moment, fixed upon other points with the helplessness and passion we have all experienced, the realization that our delight is kept in its course by some radar of history or fashion. That there is a good deal of luck, accident, "timing" and sheer chaos in these matters hardly anyone would deny. People used to say they wanted to be either rich or poor, anything but shabby-genteel, and in the same way a state of extremity is perhaps to be sought in the arts. Attacks upon great work have very nearly the same weight as praise—*bon chat, bon rat.* It is a painful but honorable destiny to be laughed at, scorned as a madman, slandered as immoral or irresponsible or dangerous. Even refusal, being entirely ignored, has in its own way a certain cold and bony beauty.

The notion of a large or small masterpiece lying about unnoticed—a Vermeer in the hayloft—has always stirred men's hearts. To be attacked or to be ignored offer at the least certain surprising possibilities for the future; the work may be dramatically discovered or excitingly defended, re-claimed. The common and lowly fate of most books is shabby gentility. They are more or less accepted, amiably received—nearly everyone is kind about effort and genial in the face of a completed task—and then they are set aside, misplaced, quietly and firmly left out, *utterly forgotten*, as the bleak phrase has it. This is the dust.

The dust seems to have settled rather quickly upon the works of Christina Stead. Her name means nothing to most people. The title of one of her novels, *The House of All Nations*, occasionally causes an eye to shine with cordiality and it may be noted that good things have been heard about this book even if it is not possible to remember precisely what they are. Is it perhaps a three-decker affair by a North-ern European once mentioned for the Nobel Prize? The title of her great novel, *The Man Who Loved Children*, doesn't sound reassuring either; the title is in fact, one could remark, not good enough for the book, suggesting as it does a satisfaction with commonplace ironies. (But no title could give a preview of this unusual novel.)

At the present time none of Christina Stead's work is in print. Her name never appears on a critic's or journalist's list of novelists, she is not a "well-known woman writer"; she has written about finance, about Salzburg, Washington, Australia and yet neither place nor subject seem to call her image to the critical eye. Upon inquiring about her from her last American publisher, the information came forth with a *tomba oscura* note: all they had was a *poste restante*, Lausanne, Switzerland, 1947. The facts of her biography seem to be that she is Australian, has lived all over Europe, and lived in America for some time and may still do so. She is, as they say, not in the picture, not right now at least, and therefore one cannot learn much about her past or her future. Yet when *The Man Who Loved Children* appeared in 1940, Rebecca West said on the front page of *The New York Times Book Review* that Christina Stead was "one of the few people really original we have produced since the First World War." Statements of that kind are not a rarity in the public press: the novelty of this one is that it is true. The dust, grimly, meanly collecting, has fallen upon a work of sheer astonishment and success.

The Man Who Loved Children has not been completely buried—it has a small and loyal band of friends. Yet that quaint locution is misleading, because it makes the book sound like a fine but frail old lady living in retirement and occasionally appearing for tea with the selected few. *The Man Who Loved Children* is not a small, perfect, witty book, but a large, sprawling, vigorous work marked by a novelistic, story-telling abundance, the wonderful richness of character and texture the critics are always irritably demanding. It is all this, all story and character and truth and directness, and yet it has been composed in a style of remarkable uniqueness and strength, of truly radical power and authenticity. This book is a genuine novel in the traditional meaning of the term; it is a story of life, faithfully plotted, clearly told, largely peopled with real souls, genuine problems; it is realistically set, its intention and drive are openly and fully revealed; it is also a work of absolute originality.

There has never been anyone in American literature like the great, talkative, tearful, pompous, womanish father, Samuel Clemens Pollitt. Sam is a bureaucrat of the office and the home; he has one of those greedy and restless minds that takes in and chews up everything in sight, like a disposal unit attached to the sink. He expresses himself vividly and tirelessly; his conversation is a rich mash of slogans, baby talk, snatches of old songs, remembered bits of information and nonsense. His very glands secrete his own special cant, his own mixture of self-loving exuberance, sensuality, windy idealism, nature lore, and public service. Pollitt works as a naturalist in Washington, D.C., in the employment of the government. Perhaps one could not seriously describe *The Man Who Loved Children* as a political novel, but in its vastly suggestive way it has something to do with Washington and with politics. It is not easy to imagine Sam Pollitt in any other situation except the one he has here. His freewheeling, fantastic talents, his active but moderately proportioned ambitions, his dignity and his moralizing fit like a glove his government-post life; a bureaucracy can use his blandly conniving and optimistic nature and assure him a well-settled if not remarkable career. Although he has some specialized knowledge, he is roundly and exhaustively general, like an encyclopedia. His wife sees him as a sort of force who has come into his career, his marriage, his self-satisfaction by the back door. He is "a mere jog-trot, subaltern bureaucrat, dragged into the service in the lowest grades without a degree, from mere practical experience in the Maryland Conservation Commission, and who owed his jealousy-creating career to her father's influence in the lobbies of the capital."

Sam Pollitt's overwhelming cantish vitality is probably not a political thing in itself, but it comes from the lush underside, the slushy, rich bottom soil of the political terrain. His every sentence is a speech to his public, his family is a sort of political party to be used, fulsomely praised, and grotesquely subjected to uplifting sermons. He is literally swollen with idealistic feelings and self-love, with democratic statement and profound self-seeking. He is as fertile of lofty sentiments as he is of children. His little ones clamor about him, blushing and laughing, like an office force, working away, pretending to be playing all the while. Here is an example of Pollitt's fatherly method of expressing himself to his brood:

> "This Sunday-Funday has come a long way . . . it's
> been coming to us, all day yesterday, all night from the
> mid-Pacific, from Peking, the Himalayas, from the fishing
> grounds of the old Leni Lenapes and the deeps of the
> drowned Susquehanna, over the pond pine ragged in the
> peat and the lily swamps of Anacostia, by scaffolded
> marbles and time-bloodied weatherboard, northeast, north-
> west, Washington Circle, Truxton Circle, Sheridan
> Circle to Rock Creek and the blunt shoulders of our
> Georgetown. And what does he find there this morning
> as every morning, in the midst of the slope, but Tohoga
> House, the little shanty of Gulliver Sam's Lilliputian
> Pollitry—Gulliver Sam, Mrs. Gulliver Henny, Lagubrious
> Louisa, whose head is bloody but unbowed, Ernest the

calculator, Little Womey . . . Saul and Sam the boy-twins
and Thomas-snowshoeeye, all sun-tropes that he came
galloping to see."

Henny Pollitt, the sour mother of Sam's children, is a
disappointed daughter of a good and prosperous Maryland
family. She is always in debt, always lazy, untidy, hysterical.
Although created upon the familiar lines of the disappointed
and disagreeable wife, Henny seems completely without
antecedents of the literary sort. She is grand and terrifying
and inexplicably likeable as she mutters to herself, plays
patience, swills tea all day, and screams at the children. As a
mother, Henny seems to experience only the most rudi-
mentary maternal feelings; she is as verbose as her detested
husband; she is sloppy, mysterious, shabby, a convincing
character made up of fantastic odds and ends, leathery
grins, stained fingers, squalid lies and brutal hopes. Where
Sam presents his family the fruits of his endless moralizing,
his flow of nonsense, proverb and hypocrisy, Henny gives
them day in and day out the hatred and insult of her heart,
the chagrin, anger, poverty, ugliness and rudeness of the
world as she knows it. When she goes downtown she returns with tales of an adventure in a street car and "a dirty
shrimp of a man with a fishy expression who purposely
leaned over me and pressed my bust . . ." or outrageous
descriptions of people:

to whom she would give the go-by, or the cold shoulder,
or a distant bow . . . or a polite good-day, or a black look,
or a look black as thunder, and there were silly old roosters
. . . filthy old pawers, and YMCA sick chickens . . .
and all these wonderful creatures, who swarmed in the
streets, stores, and restaurants of Washington, ogling, leer-
ing, pulling, pushing, stinking, overscented, screaming and

boasting, turning pale at the black look from Henny, ducking and diving, dodging and returning, were the only creatures that Henny ever saw.

Henny's fights with her husband are epics of insult, suffering and sordid vitality. But there is no way of scoring a point on Sam because he is made of words and will not bleed. After a nightmare family collision he goes right on with his imitations of various accents, his horrible but somehow admirable begetting of children, his exploitation and yet honest enjoyment of these children, his reminiscences. No matter what has happened he sleeps comfortably, his bedside table littered with "pamphlets from the Carnegie Peace Foundation, scientific journals, and folders from humanitarian leagues."

The Man Who Loved Children is sordid and bitter. In it Henny commits suicide, one of the little boys shows his feeling about life by hanging himself in effigy, the step-daughter, Louie, is worked like a horse by the entire household, Aunt Bonnie is exploited and maltreated in the same fashion. The father's oily vanity and ghastly pawings, the mother's lies and shabby dreams: such is actual material of this novel. The grim unfolding of the drama is, nevertheless, done in such a magical, abundant, inventive manner that the reading is a pleasure from beginning to end. The dialogue is realistic and plausible and at the same time humorous, original and exciting in a way that is hardly inferior to Joyce. Sometimes the language is more nearly that of England than of America: people "post parcels," drink tea morning, noon and night, have "elevenses," etc. Still the reader does not find these English turns objectionable—they seem merely another example of the author's incredible gift for amusing and vivid and interesting language. The real triumph of the book is Pollitt. He is modern, sentimental, cruel and as sturdy as a weed. There is no possibility of destroying him. After every disaster, he shoots back up, ready with his weedy, choking sentiments. In the end he is preparing to go on the radio with his "Uncle Sam Hour" and it is inconceivable that the adventure should fail. On the other hand, it will be the tough flowering of all Pollitt's coarse reality.

The Man Who Loved Children is Christina Stead's masterpiece, but all of her work is of an unusual power. *The House of All Nations* is an excellent, interesting novel, large in scale, intelligent, and splendidly detailed. In a novel like *The Salzburg Tales* one can literally say there is talent to burn, and the talent *is* burned in it. These beautifully composed tales are told by people of all sorts and nationalities who are in Salzburg to see the annual presentation of Hofmanstael's *Everyman*. It cannot be called a complete success and yet it would have taken anyone else a lifetime to produce such a strangely gifted failure. *The Salzburg Tales* is long, stately, impressive and unreadable. Her last novels, *For Love Alone* and *Letty Fox*, are also unusual and considerable works. It would be nearly impossible to start out with this author's prodigious talent for fiction and end up without writing something of its own peculiar force and distinction.

In the vast commerce of fame and reputation certain authors are pushed to the front of the counter like so much impatient, seasonal merchandise. It is idle to complain about this and in trying to put Christina Stead's work back on the market one need not insist that she replace anyone, even though there are some highly qualified candidates for retirement. A reminder of her existence should be advertisement enough, especially in the case of such a "genuine article."

1955

5 / *Memoirs, Conversations and Diaries*

Alain, the philosopher and writer, arrives first, Valéry two or three minutes later. "Les deux illustres," meeting for the first time, introduced by Henri Mondor, sit down and begin to order luncheon. Valéry, refusing the duck in favor of the meat, remarks, "Without meat, you would have with you only *M. Néant.*" Alain professes himself able to eat anything, adds that because of his teaching at the Normale he drinks very little, except sometimes milk. Valéry also likes milk, he explains, but goes to excess only with coffee. And then Alain, unable to restrain himself another moment: "*Avez-vous travaillé, ce matin, Orphée?*" (Italics mine.) Yes, Valéry works in the morning and at eleven o'clock his work for the day is finished.

A note by Clive Bell in the *Symposium** collected in honor of T. S. Eliot's sixtieth birthday: "Between Virginia [Woolf] and myself somehow the poet became a sort of 'family joke': it is not easy to say why." In the same collection, an essay by Desmond Hawkins: "I recall an afternoon tea in the early 1930's. I am the only guest and my host

* *Symposium.* Compiled by Richard March and Tambimuttu.

is a 'distinguished literary figure.' . . . I affect to despise
the great man, *of course.* . . ." (Italics mine.)

The night boat from Calais chugs along confidently,
taking us, in the *hommage* as in the cuisine, from the French
soufflé to the English cold veal.

We hardly know how to approach these "minutes" of the
luncheons between literary men in France, those "Mardis"
of Mallarmé's, those evenings at Magny's restaurant in the
Goncourt *Journals* where Saint-Beuve and Gautier with a
mysterious and almost painful genius still *exist* on the page,
neither life exactly nor fiction, but like one of those dreams
in which dead friends, with their old crumpled smiles and
grunts, their *themes*, meet you turning a corner.

About Valéry, Mallarmé or Gide you may pluck the same
berry from a dozen different vines. An occasion is not recorded by a singular guest of some peculiar stenographic
energy, an observant dilettante with no other literary occupation to fill his time; no, breaking up at midnight, *everyone*
goes home, not to rest, but to his *journal intime*, his bulging
diary. If he is Gide he will ponder himself upon the occasion,
if he is another he will "write up" Gide. Abundant com-
parisons are thus left for posterity: you may read Roger
Martin du Gard's "Notes on André Gide"—opening line in
1913, *At last I have met André Gide!*—or Gide's musings in
his journal on the meetings with Martin du Gard.

The information above on the first meeting of Alain and
Valéry is taken from a current copy of the recently revived
La Nouvelle NRF. At the beginning, M. Mondor informs us
that this same event, this "déjeuner chez Lapérouse," was
committed to print by Alain himself and appeared in the *old*
NRF in 1939. M. Mondor, robust meeter and recorder, has

also written on the first meeting of Valéry and Claudel and even the great "premier entretien" of Mallarmé and Valéry. His document on the latter begins with the information gleaned from the Alain conference: "Paul Valéry, almost every day, after eleven o'clock in the morning liked to rest from his work." It is by repetition and excess that a national eccentricity is recognized.

This overloaded pantry of memory and dialogue has a genuine literary and historical fascination—and delights of an unnameable sort: the pleasure of frayed picture albums, where no surprise is expected, and still one's heart skips a beat as he looks yet another time at the old faces, the eyes squinting in the sunlight. In France no hint of moderation nags this appetite. Not a word is lost in the afternoon dreaminess, not an accent of Mallarmé's swirls off to oblivion with the pipe smoke in that apartment on the rue de Rome, not even a silence is drowned in the punch, which, you may read in countless sources, is brought in quietly at ten o'clock by Mme. Mallarmé and her daughter. Dining almost anywhere, they have hardly unfolded the table napkins before Valéry is saying, "To read, to write are equally odious to me." Like Napoleon's hat, these remarks have a national, historical life of their own; a schoolboy would know them any place. But this man who hates to read and to write does not then, as an American might expect, speak of women or sports, but of his feelings of dizziness and fatigue after the first performance of Jarry's *Ubu Roi!* If women are mentioned at all, it is hardly what we mean when we say "they talked about women." Instead Valéry remembers Heine's witticism: "All women who write have one eye on the page and another on some person, with the exception of the Countess of Hahn who has only one eye."

In France not only literary people but the civic powers display a ready courtesy and appreciation of artistic citizens which to their English and American partners must appear almost idolatrous. Our artists *openly* wish such recognition only when they are in a sick mood of persecution or drunkenly blowing their own horns in a way they will regret the next morning. Wandering about Paris, foreigners of a literary mind think, "The Avenue Victor Hugo, that you might expect . . . but the *rue Apollinaire*, and so soon!" Regretfully we remember those Washington Square ladies who tried in vain to get a corner named after Henry James.

It is very difficult for the English and Americans to compose a respectable *hommage*, to spend a lifetime or even a few prime years on private memoirs, even comfortably to keep a journal, a diary. For these activities the French have a nearly manic facility and energy, but when we grind away at this industry it is as if we were trying to make perfume out of tobacco juice. Every sort of bruising stumble lies in wait; you observe one law of social morality only to break another. No matter where one turns the ground of possibility weakens and the writer sinks into an indiscretion at the best, nearly a crime at the worst. Reverence, which the French display without stint, seeing it a privilege, a mark of grace, to serve, to draw near, to be a witness, seems to us to impugn honesty and self-respect. If we cannot do this for the Virgin, the Saints, without an exotic act of the will, how shall we be expected to do it for a mere author of secular dramas? Art is a profession, not a shrine. And even if one does not hesitate to make a fool of himself, there are others to consider. By immoderate praise, rash compliments, one may seriously offend the modesty and reasonable expectations of the great person, who will be thrown into embarrassment by the suspicion of flattery. The fear of toadying is an overwhelming obstacle to the production of an *hommage*.

Nevertheless, we do have a great English classic in this vein; one can say it outdoes the French, that when all the memories of Gide and Valéry are at last gathered together —if an end to that enterprise can be imagined—even then they will be mere fragments by the side of Boswell's *Johnson*. Yet it is remarkable about this work of genius that, though it is known and loved to a fabulous degree, the spectacle of its coming into being has always struck a great many right-thinking readers as repellent. Even a schoolgirl must shrink with disgust from that loathsome young man, Boswell, "buttering up" Dr. Johnson, hanging about his coattails like an insurance salesman after a policy, opening up topics and then with a diseased lack of pride rushing home to write down the answers, as though he wished somehow himself to partake of Johnson's magnificence, to insinuate his own disturbing image on the screen of history. Dr. Johnson is treasured, but odium attaches to his giddy memorialist. Grateful as readers have always been for the book, they cannot imagine themselves stooping to this peculiar method of composition. Until fairly recently Boswell seemed both repugnant and insignificant—everyone knows Dr. Johnson thought his friend missed his chance for immortality by not having been alive when "The Dunciad" was written. And one would have thought the amazing longevity of the Boswell family's shame about this member would have been modified by the undying popularity of his great work. Still they seemed to think: that fourth bout of gonorrhea fully recorded elsewhere by this dog—that is our kinsman! This other thing brings credit only to Dr. Johnson who, unfortunately, is not even a connection of the Boswell family.

Boswell is a stray—he arrived without antecedents and departed without descendants. Anyone who wishes to see the strain we feel before the blank page of veneration may examine the previously mentioned *Symposium* in honor of Eliot's sixtieth birthday. This collection is one long stutter, not about Eliot's greatness, but before the unique and almost revolutionary act of proclaiming this greatness in anything except an "objective" critical essay. From the first a profound inexperience is displayed in the very organization of the project; the editors have been so bold as to reveal the difference between the abstract request and the difficult response. The preface promises a *personal* book, *private* impressions, actual meetings and so on, but what we have is a group of essays which might, with a few exceptions, appear any time. The only rarity of the work is geographical: the comments by people who have not even met Eliot come not only from England and Europe, but from Bengal, Ceylon and Greece. Perhaps there is another peculiarity— two of the essays are not primarily about Eliot, but about Pound and Irving Babbitt. No one would wish to see this sort of thing increased and multiplied. It is very clearly "against the grain." The fear of toadying is so great nearly everyone celebrates Eliot's birthday as he would celebrate his own, quietly, secretly, hardly mentioning it for fear someone would think he wanted something.

Recently, when Edmund Wilson's "critical memoir" on Edna Millay appeared one heard some literary people expressing a giggly embarrassment. Watch out, there's something *personal* here! We may breathlessly read this document, but we feel obliged in our critical souls to discount it. After all, Wilson seems to have had an "attachment" for his subject and literature is a court where personal knowledge keeps you off the jury.

In the diary, the private journal, one is relieved of the problem of seeming to debase himself in an undemocratic way before his equals or superiors, but another and more crushing burden of conscience cramps the fingers. This is the fear of outrageous vanity, of presuming to offer simply *one's own ideas* and moods, speaking in one's natural voice, which may appear—any number of transgressive adjectives are exact: boastful, presumptive, narcissistic, indulgent. There is no doubt that the diarist is the most egotistical of beings; he quite before our eyes ceases to take himself with that grain of salt which alone makes clever people bearable. Even the most gifted of men must in his own circle be "just like everyone else," not standing upon his accomplishments, but putting them aside like an old smoking jacket worn in private. The unhesitating self-regard of Gide's *Journals* would involve us in so much pain, so great an effort to strike the right note between merely rattling away on "trivialities" and recording "serious" feelings that it will hardly seem worth the while to most exceptional writers. Amateurs, like Pepys, not really writers at all, have the advantage. Our most interesting American and English journals are usually short essays or narratives on various themes, composed with the care, craft and solemnity of any other public performance; too much of the free, flowing "I" is bad taste. (On this question of the modesty we value so highly, I have heard an extremely intelligent Englishman say that E. M. Forster's relative lack of productivity was due to his not wanting to "lord it over" some of his old and dear friends by constantly and successfully appearing before the public as a novelist. Already, with Forster's reputation, things were bad enough!) In the private journal, that inscrutable scribbler, Boswell, again comes to mind. He cared terribly about literature and was at great pains to polish his style, but fortunately Boswell never got the idea. He wrote as an amateur, giving off accounts of himself so vivid and outrageous one would believe them written by an enemy, if it were not clear at every turn that they are composed with adoration: Boswell's own matchless enthusiasm for his adventures and thoughts. There are enough hints to show how tedious Boswell would have been as a self-conscious English man of letters, in good command of himself and his reputation, thoughtful of the decencies, of pride, of moderation. In spite of his efforts to achieve these qualities, Boswell hadn't the vaguest notion what they were about. There is something nearly insane in his spontaneity.

The *hommage* and an individual's account of his own nature and life are interesting, but they have hardly any of that sinful appeal of those conversations, moments in the lives of famous or infamous persons, taken down and arranged by another. The purpose of the *hommage* is to praise, the usual practice of the diarist is to look inward; but the memoir is concerned with the external, meant to reveal, to pin down others. Unless one has met a number of famous people or endured an historic moment, he cannot in the fullest sense even write his memoirs—"Memoirs of a Nobody," the title signifies an irony. The art of presenting, analyzing, recording living persons is, with us, protected and isolated by countless moral spears and spikes. The very fact that one is in a position to observe for posterity is all the more reason why he should decently refuse to do so.

The motives behind this form of historical writing are felt to be unwholesome.

Drummond's *Conversations with Ben Jonson* are a very queer moment in our literature. Still, surpassingly strange as these conversations are, they are extremely "English." They are brief—one doesn't go too far in laboring to preserve even what such a man as Ben Jonson said; people will think you have nothing else to do. Their "manliness" and "objectivity" are great; nothing feminine or gushingly interested like Boswell is involved because Drummond and Jonson did not even like each other! Drummond thought Jonson "a great lover and praiser of himself, a contemner and scorner of others," and was not disqualified as a disinterested recorder by even so much as a high opinion of Jonson's literary work since he believed this man "excelleth only in a translation." Jonson, as a guest, could not proceed without hesitation to name what he thought of Drummond and so confined himself to the mild grumble that his host's verses "smelled too much of the Schools." It is not hard to imagine what Jonson truly thought of Drummond when we read what he had to say these evenings about absent contemporaries: Donne, for not keeping the accent, deserved hanging; Daniel was jealous of him [Jonson]; Drayton feared him; Beaumont "loved too much himself and his own verses"; Raleigh employed the best wits in England to write his history; Sir Philip Sidney had pimples; of his own wife, well, "five years he had not bedded with her." Even if we did not know Jonson to be a great and lovable genius, a profound and generous critic elsewhere, we could say at least that his remarks have a quality dear to us, *honesty*. Jonson is aware, with his violent outspokenness, of a kind of need to remind the listener of this trait; he says, "of all the styles he loved most to be named honest."

Having thus enlisted our certainty that he is no flatterer, he then, complex being, falls into a terrible error: he says that of his honesty he "hath one hundred letters so naming him." After this we are immediately led back to a bit of sympathy for the irritated Drummond. A gentleman must right things in such unmanageable cases. These conversations are altogether weird.

The nearest thing in English to the Goncourts is De Quincey—his extraordinary impressions of the Lake Poets, which can hardly be excelled for style, brilliance of observation, skill in narration, and for overwhelming psychological wisdom. However, they are not much like the Goncourts because of their unique tenderness and their striking innocence of worldliness. Grasmere is one thing, Paris another; in Paris you dine with Gautier at the Princess Mathilde's, here you walk twenty miles in the rain with Dorothy and William Wordsworth. The lonely hills nourish eccentricity, not scandal. Noble and loving as they are, De Quincey's impressions provoked resentment in Wordsworth, Southey, and those of Coleridge's relatives living at the time of publication. They do indeed have their tragic moments: that horrible lodging in London where Coleridge lay in the pain and confusion of laudanum, wretchedly facing his series of lectures at the Royal Institute. They do not lack comedy, either. De Quincey adored Wordsworth, still, "useful as they proved themselves, the Wordsworthian legs were certainly not ornamental." And then this distinguished poet also had a remarkable narrowness and droop about the shoulders which caused Dorothy, walking behind him, to exclaim, "Is it possible—can that be William? How very mean he looks!" Southey may have felt his calm, regular habit of life, his immense energy, his library of beautifully bound books were a bit too faithfully described by De Quincey; the description suggests an overgrowth of secondary literary powers which crowd out the more messy ones of the first magnitude. Nevertheless the genius of everyone, and most of all of De Quincey himself, is brilliantly served by these essays. We would not for anything be without that picture of Wordsworth cutting the pages of one of Southey's lovely books with a greasy butter knife.

In De Quincey and Boswell's *Johnson* there is hardly a hint of "sex"—the subjects are all extremely eccentric in their lack of concentration on this instinct. Our own age is even more prudish in this respect; conversational and fictional freedom has increased, but in memoirs and portraits the license has been nearly revoked so that one gets roundabout psychoanalytical hints based upon facts which are not revealed. It would be very difficult for us to write, without somehow turning it into an ambiguity or a joke, "At last I have met André Gide," but we can hardly imagine the malice of writing, "I have met Gide, but he was distracted by the sight of a beautiful young boy on the beach . . ." An interesting scene of this sort occurs in Roger Martin du Gard. He says that he showed his diary to Gide and Gide was fascinated by it. Spender's friendly and very circumspect portraits of living people were by some considered "scandalous." An author would probably be outlawed for *keeping in his mind*, to say nothing of his journal, the following quotation from Flaubert found in the Goncourt work:

When I was young my vanity was such that if I found myself in a brothel with friends, I would choose the ugliest girl and would insist upon lying with her before them all without taking the cigar out of my mouth. It was no fun at all for me; I did it for the gallery.

The peculiar sanctity that surrounds our image of Flaubert, the unequaled purity of the man and his art, are not altered by this naked bit of anecdote.

Frank Harris, who clearly modeled his volumes on the Goncourts', is, one gathers, either in oblivion or, when remembered, in disrepute. This ineffable being has certain qualifications as a "portraitist," but they are nearly all erased by his incurable English, or American, moralizing. Harris is extremely sensitive to an "opportunity"; at a meeting he approaches the celebrity with the dignified and plausible expectancy of a relative at a promising deathbed. He does not pretend to be disinterested, or himself a mere nothing; but he can say in all honesty that he *cares*. And this is true: he is passionately interested in famous people. His "coverage" is wide and international; his narration of anecdote and description of character are entertaining, even if he does like to frill the edges with "winebearers at the banquet of life," and to add all sorts of conversational pockets which seem designed merely to repeat his own name. "Do you see that, Frank?" or "I will tell you a story, Frank." Harris's great trouble is that he never misses a chance to point out a "flaw" in his subject's discourse. One gets not only Shaw's very interesting claim for his own dramatic Caesar over Shakespeare's, but Harris's long-winded defense of Shakespeare against Shaw. Harris wants you to know he will not hesitate to seek out the great *and* will not allow the greatest of them to get by with "nonsense." Without indicating his refusal to agree or to practice an amiable silence, perhaps he could not have justified his exorbitant pursuit. This is very nearly fatal both for the drama and the humor of his portraits. Here is a bit of nightmare dialogue from the Goncourts, the kind of entry that gives a frightening life to their record:

Taine: ". . . In the town of Angers, they keep such a close watch on women there is no breath of scandal about a single one of them."
Saint-Victor: "Angers? But they are all pederasts. . . ."

Harris would almost certainly have followed this mad moment with: "Permit me, but I have made a special trip to Angers and both of you are stupidly wrong."

Should anyone in English wish to rival the Goncourts? Far from laboring to add more to this kind of "history," perhaps we should find the enjoyment of the Goncourt classic a guilty passion. Henry James was deeply shocked by the appearance of this work. It seemed to him an appalling occupation, every instance of it, from the brothers' account of their contemporaries to Edmond's notes on the death of Jules. Their carrying on the journal is "a very interesting and remarkable fact," but "it has almost a vulgarly usual air in comparison with the circumstance that one of them has judged best to give the document to the light." James cannot abide these "demoralized investigators," he is horrified by their picture of a grumpy and petty Saint-Beuve and points out with a cry that the thirty volumes of Saint-Beuve's *Causeries du Lundi* "contain a sufficiently substantial answer to their account of the figure he cut when they dined with him as his invited guests or as fellow-members of a brilliant club." James is not only solicitous for the artists, but for the Goncourts' maid whose bitter adventures are related, and for certain women of the world: "If Madame de Païva was good enough to dine, or anything else, with, she was good enough either to speak of without brutality or to speak of not at all." And the Princess Mathilde: "He stays in her house for days, for weeks together, and then portrays for our entertainment her person, her clothes, her gestures . . . relating anecdotes at her expense . . . the racy expressions that passed her own lips." James has, from my reading of the charming entries on the Princess Mathilde, a really cloistered notion of "racy expressions," but his objections are not trifling. They are painfully serious and worthy, as one must recognize even when he has just closed his copy of the *Journals* and pronounced them a delight. All of the people are now dead and those who do not survive by their art or historical significance are dead completely, except as they live on for the occasional Goncourt fan or in other documents of the period. Some lively creatures would, no doubt, choose immortality on any terms rather than face the utter oblivion of their names. Yet we do not know this for a certainty; the question cannot even be truly put to the sufferer, since the permanence of a portrait, vicious or pleasing, cannot be known for a long time. A shrewd person might even say: If the book is a masterpiece I don't mind being atrociously present, because even mediocrities or cads, brilliantly drawn, have a kind of grandeur—but if it is second-rate, leave me out!

In England and America where the temptation to the direct use of actual personages is so buried in hesitation, where so much seems to forbid, the practice may be attended by malice and deliberate distortion; some goddess of revenge and brutality may in fact hold the hand of the muse of history. Nevertheless, writers and readers alike have a rich interest in the living personality, an interest which does not blush even before the squalid or ludicrous revelation. If we do not practice the memoir or diary with unfaltering confidence, we have the *roman à clef* and satires like Pope's. These forms are allowed to be far more brutal than mere reportage; in the latter a certain body of fact must be observed; accuracy is all. In the novel or satire, every effort is made to identify without actually naming the fleshly reality, but once the identity is clear no restraints at all are put upon the free exercise of a malicious imagination. The author can pick and choose as he likes, exaggerate, invent; indeed he is obliged to swell here and shrink there from the necessity of creating a "character," which cannot have the exact fullness and queerness of life, but must be "exposed" more neatly, according to the demands of art. This method is less useful for "history," but it is brilliantly effective in inflicting an injury upon the living. The poor victim cannot say he has been falsely reported, since it is his very soul which is being examined; grimy motives and degrading weaknesses he has never expressed are gaily attributed to him by the satirist. Almost anyone, in his lifetime, would prefer the "pinning down" of the Goncourts to the crucifixion of "The Dunciad."

Yet even with contemporary silence the sensitive celebrity cannot keep posterity in hand. In a highly industrialized society "research" is an honorable calling. Politeness and decency have left us nothing of Emily Dickinson's swoons or suspicious flutters, still ladies and gentlemen coming later can hypothecate depths of perverse commitment about which one can at best only be an agnostic—like the after life these hypotheses cannot be proved true or false from on-the-spot accounts. The scholar can do anything he likes with Walt Whitman, or rest Herman Melville on a bed of Oedipal nails that would puncture the sleep of the most thick-skinned artist. Posterity, dipping into *Harper's Bazaar*, the *New York Times* "Interviews" and so on, will find a mute and inglorious Faulkner, a kittenish Marianne Moore, a sober Dylan Thomas—perhaps there will not even be a word, but only a picture memorializing an Allen Tate of granite solemnity and dignity, a mutely beautiful Katherine Anne Porter, a schoolmaster with a beard named Randall Jarrell. From our serious periodicals it will be learned that our literary men, and also those of the past, had no life at all: they lived and died as a metaphor. But living people, even thousands upon thousands of students, know our writers, and know them first-hand, to be fantastically interesting and—who would dispute it?—often *fantastic*. Our squeamishness and glorification of privacy may be paid for by a blank. Even a bureaucrat or a play producer might, if he gave thought to it, hesitate to enter history by way of those "profiles" and cover-stories which have become an unyielding bore of joshing flattery, whose only purpose may be to keep literary lawyers busy and neighborly researchers employed in the piling up of a benign lump of fact.

It was clear that something new was needed—nobody is *that* dull, the harried editor heard in his dreams. This something was found, a new, a fearful and quite unprecedented growth, a pioneer and monstrous crossbreeding of indifference and total recall: the *New Yorker* "article" on Hemingway. Before this it seemed never to have occurred to us that brute sound, as it were, might be a novelty, that "pieces" may after all simply be made with words, any words, if they have been truly uttered by a person of some celebrity. One would have expected these offerings to be signed with tiny initials, indicating a stenographer, or better by a few steel tracings of a machine not yet on the market, but showing in its simplicity and efficiency every possibility of easy mass production. In France a person would be guillotined for such an invention, and the very idea of this article was an invention, perhaps in the dawn of time related to the interview or the conversation, but in itself bearing no more relation to those than a cough to a song recital. By comparison, Aubrey's duchesses who "died of the pox" seem sweetly remembered.

Gorky's reminiscences of Tolstoy—a masterpiece. If anyone today were capable of composing this exalted work about a living genius, he would become so befuddled, so bent and harassed with accusation, so fearful of putting in and leaving out, it would be sensible economy to leave off altogether and return to "creative" work. What to do with himself in the reminiscence? Shall he admit his own existence or is that an unpardonable self-assertion? And isn't it putting it on a bit to pretend to "know" the marvelous being when there are so many others who have known him longer and "better."

To these moral and aesthetic questions there is no answer. Meanwhile there is always, instead, *publicity*—so easy to swallow, so difficult to remember a moment later.

1953

Lives

6 / *The Life and Death of Caryl Chessman*

They rode together in harmony, Abraham and Isaac, until they came to Mount Moriah. But Abraham prepared everything for the sacrifice, calmly and quietly; but when he turned and drew the knife, Isaac saw that his left hand was clenched in despair, that a tremor passed through his body—but Abraham drew the knife. Then they returned again home, and Sarah hastened to meet them, but Isaac had lost his faith. No word of this had even been spoken in the world, and Isaac never talked to anyone about what he had seen, and Abraham did not suspect that anyone had seen it.   Kierkegaard, *Fear and Trembling*

The "abominable and voluptuous act known as *reading the paper*," Proust called it. In a bleary, addicted daze I followed the last years in the life of Caryl Chessman and, with increasing interest—or *consumption*, perhaps one should call the taking in of the flesh and blood of a person through the daily press—his last months. After the shock of his pointless execution, after his exit from the front pages, Chessman still did not entirely remove himself from public contemplation to make room for the young criminals who seemed to spring from the earth just as his bones were lowered into it. Even during the triumphal procession, soon after his death, of Tony and Margaret—the short, little couple, their hands raised as if in a benediction—the ghostly, beaky, droopy, heart-shaped face remained, creating one of those accidental juxtapositions whose significance is everything or nothing.

I wondered how Chessman had appeared in the newspapers during his arrest and trial as "the red light bandit." I went back to the files of the *New York Herald Tribune* and looked up the dates of his tragic history. January 23, 1948, when Chessman was arrested in a stolen car and identified as the man who made assaults on two women—there was nothing in the paper; May 18th, 1948, when he was convicted on seventeen of eighteen charges—nothing; June 25, 1948, when he was given two death sentences—no mention of the case; July 3, 1948, when, at the age of twenty-seven, he entered Death Row in San Quentin prison —blankness in the *Herald Tribune* on this matter. To the East at least, Chessman had been nonexistent as a criminal, as a case, as a doomed young man. He had to bring himself forth from the void of prison, from nothingness, from nonexistence. This condition of his nothingness, his nonexistence, makes his remarkable articulation, his tireless creation of himself as a fact, his nearly miraculous resurrection or birth —which it was we do not know—a powerfully moving human drama. With extraordinary energy, Chessman made, on the very edge of extinction, one of those startling efforts of personal rehabilitation, salvation of the self. It was this energy that brought him out of darkness to the notice of the Pope, Albert Schweitzer, Mauriac, Dean Pike, Marlon Brando, Steve Allen, rioting students in Lisbon (Lisbon!)—

and, perhaps by creating his life, Chessman had to lose it. The vigor of his creation aroused fear, bewilderment, suspicion. As he tells us in his accounts of his fellow convicts on Death Row, it is usually the lost, the cringing, the deteriorated who are finally reprieved. A man needs a measure of true life in order to be worth execution.

People on the street, talking about the case, found Chessman's energy, his articulation of his own tragic trap, his stubborn efforts on his own behalf, truly alarming. These efforts were not mitigating; indeed they were condemning. He had trained himself to sleep only a few hours a night so that he could write his books, study law, work on his case. But suppose another condemned man wanted his sleep, couldn't bother to work on his own destiny, hadn't the strength or the talent to bring himself from darkness to light—what then? Lest his very gifts save him, some people wanted him executed in order to show the insignificance of personal vigor before the impersonal law. And, true, his energy is very uncommon among habitual criminals. "Flabby, bald, lobotomized" Lepke; dreamy, paretic gangsters; depressed, deteriorated murderers; goofs putting bombs on planes. Chessman was a young hoodlum who was able, in the last decade of his life, to call upon strange reserves of strength. His early violence and his late effort at personal integration seem to have come from the same mysterious source. Life is haunted by one so peculiarly instructive, a history so full of fearful symbolism.

Cell 2455, Death Row, Chessman's autobiography, is a work of genuine and poignant interest. (Its faults as literature are those almost inevitably found in naturalistic first novels by young men who are writing from harsh experience: occasional sentimentality, strained efforts at rhetorical decoration, cultural pretentiousness. Its virtues are of

the same genre—power, natural expressiveness, authenticity.)
This is an oddly American book. The need to confess violent
thoughts is softened by the cream of despairing sentiment,
remembered hopes, perfect loves, and the incongruent
beauties of the jungle. I had not thought of reading it until
after the execution. It had not seemed likely that Chessman
would have sufficient objectivity to tell us what we wanted
to know about him; or that, if he had the intention to give
a serious picture, he would have the words at hand. Almost
unwillingly one discovers that he really had, as he said, a
great deal to tell. The life of a chronic offender, existence
reduced to chaos or ruled by tides of compulsion, reform
school, jail, parole, jail once more, and death at the end of
it—that history he is abundantly able to record.

The aim of this aching revelation was to save the author
from the gas chamber and that it did not do. Its other aim
—to picture the life of a young criminal—is accomplished
with exceptional truth. Careening cars, gun fights, arrests,
escapes, loyalties and betrayals, horror, confusion, defiance,
manic decision, hopeless cruelties: there it is. But it is not
a collage. In the center is a person, young, monstrously
careless, living in hell, acting out these sordid images and
twisted yearnings. Chessman is himself and also a national
and international phenomenon of our period. Someone like
him will be in the news tomorrow in New York, in Paris, in
Moscow. His story has an uncanny application at a hundred
points. You never doubt his existence or that of his companions, desperate boys named Tuffy or Skinny, and coarse
girls, defiantly self-debasing. These are harsh portraits, very
unlike the social worker's case history, the TV delinquents,
who cannot avoid a false tidiness and handsomeness as they
sweat to render an image not their own. The kindly, manly
interviewer, the restless kid, the nagging, hysterical parents

—the truth is so much worse than the "problem." We know convicts and condemned men are people, but we are always certain they are not the people in the movies. Their restless, self-devouring emptiness, so like our own, has an unbearably great importance because of their crimes against others and their torture to themselves. Chessman's books, particularly *Cell 2455*, and many passages from his other books about his case, could not possibly be negligible because of the information he was peculiarly able to impart. And beyond that, the fact that he, from whom nothing could have been expected, was able to write them at all is a circumstance of compelling interest. It seems to suggest that only through "art," through some difficult and utterly personal expression is reclamation and prevention possible. This is a world beyond the therapy of the basketball court, the recreation center, the social worker's hopeful sympathy. Its energy alone could only be used up in some violent dedication.

The Story: Chessman's family, his early years, are not what one would expect. He was an only child who loved his parents and was loved by them. Perhaps this love lends itself to interpretation because of his tendency to idealize his parents and his failure to make them real. About his mother: "Hallie was a dreamer, at heart a poetess with both feet firmly planted on the ground and her soft, searching blue eyes in the heavens." In any case, the affection on both sides was real and lasting. Chessman was spared the blight of neglect, abandonment, beatings, drunkenness; his severe delinquency does not easily yield its secret and the family situation is a clue to his strength rather than his weaknesses. His parents urged him to "do the right thing," to return to reform school when he had escaped and so on, but he does not record any pressure more coercive than their mere hopes and pleas. They were feeble trusting people. They believed whatever excuse their son gave for staying out all night and were always surprised and dismayed to learn he had been "getting into trouble." Chessman's schemes, his plans, his hopes, all expressed in the vigorous distortions of his own personality, were of a degree of vitality and daring beyond anything the parents could call upon. They were frail, harmless branches blown about by a genuine tornado. To the tornado, they are the idealized calm, pitiful and innocent. He defends and destroys them at the same time. After he was grown, Chessman learned that his mother was a foundling. She did not know who she was. He set out to find her. With the money he got holding up brothels, he hired a detective to trace his mother's origins. Nothing was discovered.

Early, he contracted bronchial asthma. He was nursed and protected by his parents, but in his own mind the asthma was a profound indication of weakness and shame. "The need to be strong became more demanding with each passing attack." A few years later, an attack of encephalitis left Chessman tone deaf. "The disease ravaged [his] personality as well as his physical self." This was followed by tantrums at school, cruelty, and hatred of himself because of aggressive feelings. His mother was injured in an automobile accident and became permanently paralyzed. Disasters multiplied. All the family resources were spent on the mother's illness. When Chessman was fifteen, his father attempted suicide, "with a prayer for forgiveness." The family went on the dole. With the humiliation of food packages, Chessman began his criminal activity. He told his credulous parents that he had a paper route and got up early in the morning to rob stores of provisions left outside. The dole, the food packages, the search for new doctors and new operations for the mother are pretexts for crime; he does not pretend they were more than that.

All pretexts are gradually discarded. Motivation is hidden and justification is not even attempted beyond the hunger of vanity and the compulsion of destructiveness. "He committed nine burglaries, he purchased food with forged personal checks and got, in addition to the food, a dollar or two back in cash." Because of his childhood illnesses and physical weaknesses, Chessman convinced himself that he wouldn't live long and that his thefts and forgeries would be punished by God. His guilt was relieved and, waiting as he was upon his final and eternal judgment, he could hope his parents would not discover his misdeeds. Not long after, he went to a doctor for a simple stomach ache and had his illusion of imminent death destroyed. He was told he was sound and healthy. "These words had an almost paralyzing effect. . . . They meant he wouldn't die!" His parents, after all, would have the sorrow of his disgrace. "God had no right to punish his parents for what he had done! Already they had been made to suffer too much. Already they had made too many sacrifices for him. He, alone, deserved punishment." (These are youthful sentiments, recalled later. Chessman died an atheist, rejecting religious rites and burial and saying that for him to call upon God would be hypocrisy. One of his lawyers thought this his worst trait of character.)

It is hard to avoid the thought that Chessman's conscious feelings about his parents masked other feelings of great distress to himself. Shortly after his discovery that he would have to live, he began to risk everything. And the story of his life, at the point of its greatest recklessness and violence, becomes more truthful. Self-knowledge increases, as nostalgia, adolescent emotions, acceptable fears and longings withdraw.

Cars: "That night he stole two cars and committed three burglaries." The young offender's dreams are alive with the embraces of warm, fat, forbidden cars. The car is freedom, power, exhilaration, madness. "Driving was a joyous form of creative expression. Driving made him free. Driving was his personal, triumphant accomplishment." Yet, the pleasure of driving is no greater than the joy in wrecking. ". . . he practiced driving or 'tooling' these hot heaps. He learned to corner, to broadside, to speed and snap-shift them. He purposely rolled and crashed them. He sent them hurtling through traffic at high speeds. He sought out patrol cars and motorcycle cops and taunted them into chasing him, just for the thrill of ditching them, just for the hell of it, and for practice." The car is escape—and capture. No sooner are Chessman and the other reform boys out of jail than they are in a stolen car, running through a stop light, alerting the police, who start after them and put them back in jail. The car is not stolen, altered, driven, to provide accommodation for the criminal on the run. It is wrecked just when it would be most useful. It is driven conspicuously, not stealthily.

Capture: Capture is courted with all the passionate energy that just a few weeks previously went into escape. "I stepped into a stolen car the Glendale police had staked out and was promptly arrested by two detectives with drawn guns." Or "I wanted peace and I unhesitatingly declared war to find it. I wanted to get even, to have one last defiant fling, and to go out in a blaze of ironically stolen glory." There is no meaning, no purpose, no gain. "Repeatedly we had had it impressed upon us that the road we followed led not to riches but to prison or the grave. Soon we reached the point where we were unable to justify the continuation of our collective effort without frankly admitting that our goal was merely to raise as much violent, dramatic, suicidal hell as possible. . . ."

He was put in reform school, released in April, 1937. He came home to his weak, lenient, kind parents. "The next day he was home and his homecoming was a happy one. . . . Not a word of censure did he hear. His parents' sole concern was for his future and how it could be made a success. And they were immensely pleased at how sturdy and healthy he appeared." Freedom is brief. The need to get back in conflict with the law begins almost at the prison gate, after the handshake with the paroling officer, after the lecture. Paroled in April, in May he had stolen a car and more armed robberies began. All of this culminated years later in his arrest and identification as the "red light bandit," an armed robber who flashed a red light into cars parked on "lovers' lanes," robbed the couple, and twice sexually assaulted the women. "After nine years of criminal violence and penal servitude following his release from reform school, he had come to the condemned row at San Quentin prison, twice condemned to death."

San Quentin at last. Prison is a part of the cycle; escape and capture, alternate back and forth, "naturally." Capture is rest from the manic push. The glum, exhausted face of the young outlaw is as revealing as his arrogant, excited mask during the chase. There is no sensible plan, no criminal organization; it is crime and punishment, escape and capture, parole and violation. San Quentin, the ultimate, the final, appears early in this grim dialogue. With Chessman, the exhilaration of violence gives way to extraordinary exertion in handling the fact of imprisonment.

Cruelty and threats have no meaning to men who live by

cruelty and threats. They merely provide self-justification. The desire to be strong, not to bend under punishment, keeps criminal defiance alive. "I preferred to stand on my own feet, even if it was in hell." Independence, fearlessness, distorted into horrors, have a monstrous power over the convict. Chessman certainly died with "dignity," and that was the best he could do for himself, even if his kind of fearlessness is a tragic example of strength. Even his last words make much of the crippling "courage" he had lived by. "When you read this, they will have killed me. I will have exchanged oblivion for an unprecedented twelve year nightmare. And you will have witnessed the final, lethal, ritualistic act. It is my hope and my belief that you will be able to report that I died with dignity, without animal fear and without bravado. I owe that much to myself."

The woe of his crimes and the waste of his life lay upon Chessman's soul. He feels that society does not understand the young criminal. It is his mission to explain. "It is the story of a grinning, brooding, young criminal psychopath in definitely willing bondage to his psychopathy." The fate is personal, mysterious. "My father had failed to grasp the real reason for my many clashes with authority. He would never understand what drove me. He never would be fully aware of the jungle."

And what drove him? What was the jungle? "I ventured the thought that perhaps after one spends a while in a jungle world he gets so he cannot or does not want to believe there is anything better, or that it is attainable in any case. Maybe hate has a lot to do with it. Hate for everybody, for himself."

"But there are periods of self-doubt when you know yourself for what you really are—an angry, hating, fighting *failure*. Usually then you curse your doubts and blaspheme the imagery [*sic*] of the self you see."

His history is appalling. "Yes, I have been in reform schools, jails, and prisons most of my life. Yes, I had committed many, many crimes and had ample warning of what to expect if I kept on. Yes, I had kept on nevertheless. No, I was not guilty of the crimes for which I was sentenced to death. I was not the red light bandit. . . . Yes, I would say I was not the red light bandit even if I were."

The Thing is describable but inexplicable. "I was one of the trees in this dark and forbidding forest. I knew what it meant to live beyond the reach of other men or God. I had 'proved' everything I had felt the need to prove: that I couldn't be scared or broken or driven to my knees, that I didn't give a damn. But here is where the tragedy lies: this felt need is compulsive and negative only. It is a need to prove one can do without—without love, without faith, without belief, without warmth, without friends, without freedom. This negative need to prove becomes progressively greater and greater . . . the ultimate (conscious or unconscious) need is to prove that one can do without even life itself."

How is society to heal such a desperate sickness? Chessman puts himself in the position of a leper who is also a physician. He studies his own pains and deformations; he does not find the answer. Each offender is different from every other. The salvation of the meanest or the mildest is as complicated and difficult as the life of every non-criminal man. It is tedious, discouraging, even hopeless. Society is too dull, too rigid, too tired to make the effort. We do not even want to reform the criminal because of our anger that we have sometimes tried and failed. Every account of jails, of guards and matrons seems to show that reform is not believed in or encouraged. If a man might be saved by eight hours at the piano, the warden is sure to put him in the jute mill to teach him his lesson. The senseless determination of the prison officials to keep poor Chessman from writing is one of the most depressing and telling aspects of this sad case. One of the wardens at San Quentin, admitting that Chessman was not a difficult disciplinary problem, said, "So far as I'm concerned, our only problems with him have been literary."

The case: There was a large element of the sacrificial in Chessman's execution. Even if he was absolutely guilty, the way of stating the charge and the decision to give the death penalty were severe beyond anything we are accustomed to. Further, the fact that the unusual severity of the sentence, in a case where murder was not involved or kidnapping either in any sense in which the world understands the term, could not be modified after exhaustive litigation suggests again the sacrificial and symbolic nature of the case. In Mark Davidson's study in *The Californian* he says, ". . . Chessman was not convicted of rape, because in both of the robbery-attack offenses for which he was condemned, the victims persuaded the bandit not to pursue coitus. The bandit instead had them perform *fellatio*. . . ." It has been widely suggested that Chessman's execution was society's punishment of its own perverse sexual wishes or deeds.

The mystery and force of Chessman's character were probably more outraging than the sordid crime itself. This older juvenile posed the question for which we have no answer. Why had he been a hoodlum at all? His cockiness, his loquaciousness, his cleverness, his energy, his talents only made his life more mysterious and more repulsive. His command of the word repelled the jurors. One of them twelve years later told a reporter that Chessman was just "as vicious as ever." When asked how she could know this, she replied, "After all, I seen his picture in the papers and he still has that same mean look, don't he?" He went on talking, defying, acting as his own lawyer, writing books, trying society's patience more and more. His life represents our defeat, our dread of the clear fact that we do not know how to deal with the senseless violence of the young. It is not too hard to understand organized crime, but how can you understand two young boys who kill an old couple in their candy store for a few dollars? In our rich society, the smallness of the sums for which people are killed shows a contempt for money as well as for human life. The nihilism at the bottom of Chessman's fate, his brains, what the newspapers called his "evil genius," made him a fearful and dreadful example. His cleverness undid him. His fight for his life was stubborn, cocky, pugnacious—and defiant.

In a sacrificial death, the circumstances that the mass fears and dreads and violently condemns may arouse involuntary feelings of wonder and grief in others. There was something almost noble in the steely, unyielding effort Chessman had made to define and save himself. He was a real person. He had breathed life into himself. One could only say that when he died this poor criminal was *at his best*. It was dismal to think his struggle counted for nothing. His ordeal was a tangle of paradoxes. He had spent twelve years in the death house because the law hesitated to deny him every possibility for reversal of the sentence. Those were horrible years, awaiting the answer. Would it have been better if he had been executed six months after his sentence? No, it would not have been better. And yet twelve years are twelve years, a unique suffering that cannot be denied. Somehow a justice complicated enough to delay twelve years to study the "technicalities" should have been complicated enough to refuse death simply because so many delays were legally possible. A part of the protest was a cry against rigidity and against the element of meanness in the law's refusal to place the case in a human context. And there was the *feeling* that Chessman might be innocent.

The claims for innocence: 1. The transcript of the trial was deeply impugned by the death of the court stenographer before he had transcribed more than a third of his private notes. The transcription and the enlargement were done, without Chessman's approval, by a relative of the prosecutor. 2. The description of the red light bandit, given before the arrest, did not entirely fit Chessman. 3. He was identified not in the line-up, but in handcuffs. 4. He had committed a wide variety of crimes, none of them involving attacks on women before this arrest. 5. He said he was innocent of the crimes for which he was sentenced to death.

After Chessman died in the death chamber, Governor Brown said he was sorry he had had no power to stay the execution and claimed he said this even though he was fully satisfied of Chessman's guilt. It was reported he then went for a lonely, sorrowing ride in the country. A detective who worked on Chessman's case and later married one of the victims attended the execution at San Quentin and said, when the death was at last accomplished, "I'm satisfied."

The end was reported with prodigal fullness. As I gluttonously read a dozen newspapers—a dozen newspapers all telling the same story of the gas pellets, the winks, the final lip-read goodbyes, the last struggles of the body—I remembered a hanging that had taken place in my youth. On the morning a Negro was to be hanged in the courthouse yard, other Negroes stayed at home from their work for fear of the way the wind might blow. That same morning a relation of mine went downtown to shop in a department store. The Negro who would ordinarily have been operating the elevator was at home, quietly waiting for the dangerous day to pass. My relation fell down the elevator shaft and suffered ghastly damage to her body and mind.

1960

She was melancholy, head-achy, with a slow, disciplined, hard-won, aching genius that bore down upon her with a wondrous and exhausting force, like a great love affair in middle age. Because she was driven, worn-out, dedicated, George Eliot needed unusual care and constant encouragement; indeed she could not even begin her great career until the great person appeared to help her. Strange that it should always be said of this woman of bold strength that she "was not fitted to stand alone." She waited for help, standing in the wings, ailing, thinking and feeling—speechless. She was homely, even ugly, and perhaps that accounted for some of her thoroughness and quiet determination; she was afraid of failure and rebuff. She suffered. Who can doubt that she was profoundly passionate and romantic? You cannot read her books or study her personal history, search for her character and temperament, without feeling her passionate nature immediately. It was agony not to be able to *appeal* in a simple, feminine way. Her countenance quite spontaneously brought to mind—the horse. Virginia Woolf speaks of George Eliot's "expression of serious and sullen and almost equine power" and Henry James felt himself nearly in love with the "great, horse-faced, blue-stocking." If she did not appeal, she *impressed* overwhelmingly. Her genius, her splendid power of mind, yes, but there is something powerfully affecting about her too, the fact that it was this particular woman who had the genius and the mind. When she died Lord Acton said, "It seems to me as if the sun had gone out. You cannot imagine how much I loved her."

Nothing was easy. It was always unremitting effort, "raising herself with groans and struggles." Sometimes it seems that she is at the mercy of her intelligence; she is not an argumentative woman and likes peace and affection about her. Still she had to learn German, was compelled by an inner demon to suffer through a decision about going to church with her father; she must read Spinoza, must make up her mind about difficult matters. In an almost helpless way she cared about philosophy, politics, moral issues as other women care about clothes while often wishing they needn't. Again Virginia Woolf: "the culture, the philosophy, the fame and the influence were all built upon a very humble foundation—she was the grand-daughter of a carpenter." A great deal of the drama of this bewitching life can be found in Professor Gordon Haight's edition of the first three volumes of George Eliot's *Letters*. Haight's massive scholarship, his long and brilliant work could hardly be surpassed.

George Eliot's fame was immense; her books sold well and she made money; she was a distinguished public figure; her image and spirit were ennobling without being cold or for the few. She was solid and reassuring, of a dignity as large and splendidly detailed as her solid, deep, dignified novels. It is easy to think of Queen Victoria and some people who cherish George Eliot seem to want us to think of the old, puffy-cheeked Queen. This novelist's history has al-

ways contained an instructive moral possibility. She is seen
as the supreme cultural fact demonstrating the value of
sober living, earnestness, and the brisk attention to matters
at hand of a reliable man with a family business. Serene, brilliant, responsible: there she stands in her paradoxically plain
grandeur. As one grows older this industrious, slowly de-
veloping soul becomes dear for a secret reason—for having
published her first story at the age of thirty-eight.

Still, too much is made of the respectability of a great
lover. Her most daring act, the most violent assertion of
self, was not the "marriage" with Lewes, but her marriage eighteen months after Lewes's death to Mr. Cross,
"one many years her junior and totally unknown and
obscure." Cross was probably a mistake; in all his public
appearances he is firmly on the dull side. (It is astounding
to learn in Haight that this man lived on until 1924—a
strange old coot for the Jazz Age.) George Eliot was
obviously strongly impulsive, but then many of the Vic-
torians were troubled in spirit and indulgent in habits. Even
the familiar Dickens had his love problems, Tennyson drank,
and Wordsworth had an illegitimate child. George Eliot
was certainly not Queen Victoria. She was pre-eminently an
artist, with all the irregularity of temperament and determination to do as she pleased common among such personalities. She and her husband, Lewes not Cross, are inconceivable as anything except what they were, two writers,
brilliant and utterly literary. They led the literary life from
morning to midnight, working, reading, correcting proofs,
traveling, entertaining, receiving and writing letters, planning literary projects, worrying, doubting their powers, experiencing a delicious hypochondria. The Brownings, the
Webbs, the Garnetts, the Carlyles, Leonard and Virginia
Woolf, Middleton Murry and Katherine Mansfield—the

literary couple is a peculiar English domestic manufacture, useful no doubt in a country with difficult winters. Before the bright fire at tea-time, we can see these high-strung men and women clinging together, their inky fingers touching. No "partnership" was more fantastic than that of George Eliot and George Henry Lewes. They were heroic, slightly grotesque—nearly the last thing one can imagine is that these two creatures would become a public institution. Edmund Gosse describes the great pair driving home in a victoria. "The man, prematurely ageing, was hirsute, rugged, satyr-like, gazing vivaciously to left and right; this was George Henry Lewes. His companion was a large, thickset sybil, dreamy and immobile, whose massive features, somewhat grim when seen in profile, were incongruously bordered by a hat, always in the height of the Paris fashion, which in those days commonly included an immense ostrich feather; this was George Eliot. The contrast between the solemnity of the face and the frivolity of the headgear had something pathetic and provincial about it."

Her husband: George Henry Lewes. He was witty, lively, theatrical, industrious, a very conspicuous figure in London intellectual life. Lewes sometimes went about lecturing, liked to produce and act in his own plays, and was successful as an important editor. As a literary man he displayed the same animation and variety for which he was known in the drawing rooms of his friends. To give but the slimmest idea of his production one can mention farces by the titles of *Give a Dog a Bad Name* and *The Cozy Corner*, a novel called *Rose, Blanche and Violet*, a large undertaking like the *Biographical History of Philosophy*, separate lives of Robespierre and Goethe, books on the drama, innumerable articles on literature and philosophy—this husband knew all about the pains of a life of composition. Leslie Stephen speaks of

Lewes as "one of the most brilliant of the literary celebrities of the time."

Lewes was not exactly the person a match-maker would seize upon as a suitable husband for George Eliot. There is a marked strain of recklessness and indiscretion in his charm; he was, as a temperament, extremely informal—Jane Carlyle called him "the Ape" and found him "the most amusing little fellow in the world." Lewes was not a handsome man, indeed he was "the ugliest man in London," according to Douglas Jerrold. George Eliot herself was somewhat put off by his unimportant appearance and had prejudice in that direction to overcome before she could entirely accept him. The impression he made was an odd one, well enough perhaps for literary circles but not up to snuff for conventional social life. "He had long hair and his dress was an unlovely compromise between morning and evening costume, combining the less pleasing points of both." Some idea of the relaxed standards of Lewes's circle when he was living with his first wife may be found in the following anecdote from Jane Carlyle: "It is Julia Paulet who has taken his [Lewes'] soul captive!! he raves about her 'dark, luxurious eyes' and 'smooth, firm flesh'—! his wife asked 'how did he know? had he been feeling it?' "

Lewes's first wife, Agnes, was beautiful, intelligent, and free-spirited in a literal and alarming way. To her children by Lewes she added two by Thornton Hunt, the son of Leigh Hunt. Lewes endured this fantastic intrusion for some time with a remarkable lack of rancor. Even after his "elopement" with George Eliot good relations were kept up on all sides. Henry James in his first visit to them found George Eliot in a state of great anxiety because one of Lewes's sons had been injured in an accident. She herself paid Agnes' allowance after Lewes died. The attitudes of everyone indicate a generous, unconventional spirit of the sort we are accustomed to find among artists and writers but would not demand of the "respectable" and especially not where matters of such overwhelming emotional charge are concerned. Still it was all very irregular and strange. Looking back at Lewes's pacific behavior, his endurance of suffering and humiliation, we can see a sort of prefiguration of the unusual position in which he later found himself. He was bright and sympathetic and yet there is an infinite longing in his lavish, humble love. As a husband Lewes discovered his wife's genius, or rather he "uncovered" it as one may, peeling off the surface inch by inch, uncover a splendid painting beneath. All this he did with excitement and delight, as if it were his own greatness he had come upon. The most haunting fact ever recorded about this odd man is from Charlotte Brontë: "the aspect of Lewes's face almost moves me to tears; it is so wonderfully like Emily's. . . ." Perhaps what Charlotte Brontë saw in "the Ape" was his wild and tender uniqueness, his inexplicable nature.

Suppose George Eliot had not become a famous novelist: what then would have happened to this marriage in which it was Lewes's role to guide, encourage, protect the most celebrated woman in England? Probably it would have been the same, although on a less grand and public stage; instead of the novelist, Lewes would have protected the diffident translator and essayist, soothed the tired editor. There is no doubt he was profoundly respectful of his chosen lady; he understood everything pained and precious in her nature, saw that striking union of dutifulness and imagination. They had, after all, been introduced by Herbert Spencer.

This grand alliance did not fail to irritate many people. A rival novelist, Eliza Linton, was furious about it. She thought their airs were impossible, their solemn importance not to be endured. Mrs. Linton had met George Eliot before the latter was famous and she says about her: "I will candidly confess my short-sighted prejudices with respect to this to-be-celebrated person. She was known to be learned, industrious, thoughtful, noteworthy; but she was not yet the Great Genius of her age, nor a philosopher bracketed with Plato and Kant, nor was her personality held to be superior to the law of the land. . . . She was essentially underbred and provincial. . . ."

Poor Mrs. Linton had reason to complain. She was not only a rival novelist but, you might say, a rival divorcee. "There were people who worshipped those two, who cut me because I separated from Linton. . . ." Envy and outrage make Mrs. Linton slyly fascinating. (One needn't fear corruption because of the impossibility of anyone succeeding in making George Eliot look foolish and small.) And sometimes Mrs. Linton sums it up perfectly. She writes, ". . . she had the devotion of a man whose love had in it that element of adoration and self-suppression which is dearest of all to a woman like George Eliot, at once jealous and dependent, demanding exclusive devotion and needing incessant care—but ready to give all she had in return." Also it is Mrs. Linton who has left us George Eliot gravely announcing, "I should not think of allowing George to stay away a night from me."

Leslie Stephen thinks George Eliot's powers were diminished by Lewes's efforts to shield her from criticism, to keep her in a cozy nest of approval and encouragement. But Stephen's opinion is based upon his belief that her later novels are inferior to the earlier ones. Stephen didn't much like *Middlemarch*, nor did Edmund Gosse—both preferred the early work. It is hard to feel either of these men had anything more than *respect* for George Eliot. They were formidable, learned figures, great personages themselves. Something in the Warwickshire novelist fails to attract them. They seem put off by the grandness of her reputation —it makes them uneasy, even somewhat jealous. Gosse says "we are sheep that look up to George Eliot and are not fed by her ponderous moral aphorisms and didactic ethical influence." It is Gosse's opinion that *Middlemarch* is "mechanical," it is "unimaginative satire" and "genius misapplied."

Astonishing that the truest lovers of this "ponderous" and "ethical" writer are the baroque aesthetes Proust and Henry James. And always the strange lover, Lewes, like someone from Dostoevsky taking over duties at the Priory, their house. Before his connection with George Eliot, Lewes had been mad about Jane Austen.

1955

8 / Loveless Love: Graham Greene

"Do you love me, Ticki?"
"What do you think?"
"Say it, one likes to hear it—even if it isn't true."
"I love you, Louise. Of course, it's true."

This exhausted domestic dialogue is used with remarkable power in Graham Greene's novel, *The Heart of the Matter*. Greene has stolen the trivial chatter of marriage from Noel Coward and given it an existential, neo-Catholic varnish, the high polish of fear and trembling and sickness unto death. The petulant archaisms, the white lies, are profanations of the lost ability to love; they bring moral fatigue, not satisfaction ("Say it again, darling!"). The nasty emptiness of the evening compliment ("My dear, how absurd you are. I've never known anyone with so many friends"); the anxiety that one's desperate separateness will be noticed ("He flinched a little away from her, and then hurriedly in case she had noticed lifted her damp hand and kissed the palm"); the nervous wretchedness of politeness; the anguish edging outrageous promises to provide for another's happiness ("Don't worry. I'll find a way, dear")—in all of this dry, light material Greene finds the terror of, to use Marianne

Moore's phrase, that "interesting impossibility," marriage and ideal love.

Scobie, an official in a British-governed town on the west coast of Africa, does not love his wife and so the reckless, embarrassing language of marriage, the optimistic accent, fill him with a dread of such great dimensions that each expected deception appears as a terrible crime. The vocabulary of Scobie's heart is responsibility, self-hatred, anxiety, and guilt. There is a scalding monotony and desperation in his life because of his supererogatory sense of pity. Scobie is mild, dutiful, just, a Catholic who loves God with the bitter passion that has died out in his earthly attachments. All of his secular life is contained in his reluctance to inflict pain. He suffers the agonies of the dinner table and the bedroom as if they were an immense crime against God; his wife's tears are a death sentence; her inevitable moments of ugliness fill him with the "pathos of her unattractiveness"; her absurdity, a malicious remark at her expense arouse in him a bereaved, tragic defense of the right of everyone to live without scorn. With intense seriousness he accepts the burden of her dissatisfaction as his due responsibility. With a kind of fury he compromises his deepest principles to get the money for her voyage to South Africa. After she has gone, he expects to find peace in his loneliness, in the honesty of being accountable only to himself, but, instead, and without wishing it, he becomes involved in a love affair. Again his sharpest emotion is pity; again, to avoid pain, he is brought back to the painful depths of "I love you" and "I'll never leave you." His very act of adultery is a sin which he cannot repent without dishonoring his mistress; he cannot make the required religious effort to abandon the relationship without bringing unhappiness to the woman who depends upon him. His wife returns and to please her he takes Communion, although in a state of mortal sin. His love of God and his duty to life conflict at every point. At last he commits suicide, sacrifices his soul to be relieved of the torture of sacrificing others.

Greene finds in his weary, sad sinner a great religious personality. Scobie is ordinary, inconspicuous, hiding his profound struggle behind his decent, rather colorless appearance. Apparently Greene had a figure in mind like the knight of faith, of whom Kierkegaard said, "Good Lord, is this the man? Is it really he? Why, he looks like a tax-collector!"

"I think he loved God," the priest says, after Scobie's impious death. This mystical resolution, weak and perverse as it is, is the only thing the Catholic novelist can salvage out of the modern, secular ruins in which he feels compelled to place his hero. There is this element of snobbishness in serious Catholic writers. They are bored with the regular devotions, the bland submissiveness—modern man is so much more "interesting." These writers want multiplicity, waywardness, spiritual torment, weakness and pride; they are in love with sin and intimate with spirituality only as the capacity for suffering from weaknesses. Toward the conventionally pious they are inattentive and Greene is positively churlish. Sebastian in *Brideshead Revisited* is a drunkard, neurotically enslaved to an evil German boy, and yet he is "holy." Waugh says, "He'll develop little eccentricities of devotion, intense personal cults of his own; he'll be found in the chapel at odd times and missed when he's expected. Then one morning, after one of his drinking bouts, he'll be picked up at the gate dying, and show by a mere flicker of the eyelid that he is conscious when they give him the last sacraments. It's not such a bad way of getting through one's life."

Greene, in the dramatic self-slaughter, pushes personal heresy to the limits with a greediness that is convincing neither as fiction nor as religion. His hero must be everything at once. He must not only be a sinner, but must commit the worst sin, and with paradox upon paradox, be nearer to grace than anyone else. Mrs. Scobie, a devoted Catholic, is "furiously" reprimanded by the priest for her impudence in assuming that Scobie will be damned forever. She is guilty of the most sluggish literal-mindedness.

Scobie cannot be understood, cannot be reached or commented upon in terms of psychology or theology. His feeling of responsibility to others approaches arrogance; his death is almost frivolous since it is his last act of pity for a wife whose needs are expressed, "Oh, Ticki, Ticki, you won't leave me ever, will you? I haven't got any friends—not since the Tom Barlows went away." As Mary McCarthy wrote about an earlier novel of Greene's, "One cannot imagine a character whose behavior is wholly governed by pity, and one feels that Greene, in pretending that it is possible, is being pious and insincere."

And yet, in spite of Greene's obstinate extension of one emotion, he has done a great deal with Scobie's pity, his loveless love, his anguish over the uncommitted, unmarried part of himself. *The Heart of the Matter* is interesting and serious for its plain, grim understanding of the moral pain of exaggerated sentiment, the tragic heroism of watching over another's life.

1948

"*The passenger wondered when it was that he had first begun to detest laughter like a bad smell.*"
"*. . . I suffer from nothing. I no longer know what suffering is. I have come to the end of all that, too.*"

"The boat goes no further."
". . . I am sorry, I am too far gone, I can't feel at all, I am a leper."

The passenger, a distinguished church architect named Querry, is the hero of Graham Greene's last novel, *A Burnt-Out Case*. Querry has been loved by many women; he is successful and famous—above all, *famous*. And from it he has ended up tired, morally despairing, filled with self-loathing, insisting upon his loss of feeling, his deadness. Loss of feeling? What does it mean? Fitzgerald's "Crack-up"—what is really meant, what has happened? "And then, ten years this side of forty-nine, I suddenly realized that I had prematurely cracked." The cracked plate, the burnt-out case, the reserved, evasive actually, description of some overwhelming emotional crisis. Fitzgerald: "I saw that even my love for those closest to me was become only an attempt to love . . ." Querry: "She was once my mistress. I left her three months ago, poor woman—and that's hypocrisy. I feel no pity."

Fame and emptiness. Fame burns out Querry; it surrounds him with horrors who draw near to touch or to fall in love. "Fame is a powerful aphrodisiac." Publicity, the bed sore of the fame-sick, inflicts its pains. Querry has abandoned his career and gone to a leprosy hospital in the Congo. He is at the end of the road; the boat goes no further; his vocation for building and for loving women has given out; he is empty, desperately and courageously "dead." But his fame runs along after him; he is discovered; he is exposed by a journalist; he is pursued by a European manufacturer of margarine, Rycker, who feels for the famous man the mad, easily resentful but somehow grotesquely transfigured, love made of Querry's success and their shared Catholicism. The famous architect and lover is now, in some sense, impotent. ("He told me once that all his life he had only made use of women, but I think he saw himself in the hardest possible light. I even wondered sometimes whether he suffered from a kind of frigidity.") Rycker kills the object of his over-weening curiosity, Querry, because of an imaginary infidelity. "Absurd," Querry said, "this is absurd or else . . ."

There is an absence of particularity, of the details of experience, in Querry's crack-up, just as there is in Fitzgerald. We reach the end of a great and adored man and accept the despair without any real idea of how it came to be. Curtness, coolness, even carelessness mark the mode of expression. Fitzgerald: "Sometimes, though, the cracked plate has to be retained in the pantry, has to be kept in service as a household necessity. It can never again be warmed on the stove nor shuffled with the other plates in the dishpan; it will not be brought out for company, but it will do to hold crackers late at night or to go into the ice box under left-overs." Querry in disgust: "The darkness was noisy with frogs, and for a long while after his host had said good night and gone, they seemed to croak with Rycker's hollow phrases: Grace: sentiment: duty: love, love, love." Self-condemnation, indifferent, impersonal, given out as a Confession, a general statement of sinfulness, without names or places. Art has failed to bring peace; success does not bring happiness to wives, mistresses or children.

From *Death in Venice:* Art "engraves adventures of the spirit and the mind in the faces of her votaries; let them lead outwardly a life of the most cloistered calm, she will in the end produce in them a fastidiousness, an over-refinement, a nervous fever and exhaustion, such as a career of extravagant passions and pleasures can hardly show." This is a price, perhaps, but a noble, classic fate—far from the sardonic ash-heap of Greene. Or compare Mailer's *Advertisements,* a confession in which I, at least, do not find the voice of personal suffering and so assume it was not intended. The alcoholic reserve of Fitzgerald and the manic expressiveness of Mailer show the twenty years or more that separate the personal documents. For Mailer more and more experience, more and more fame—the Congo as an assignment, perhaps, not as a retreat. "Publicity can be an acid test for virtue," Greene says. Poor Hemingway, honorifically carried to his grave by those wooden angels, the restaurant owner Toots Shor and the gossip columnist Leonard Lyons.

In *The Heart of the Matter* the weary hero faced damnation because of his unconquerable pity for the women whom destiny, capriciously, or due to his own wanting, left in his care. Pity is way beyond Querry. He doesn't want to pretend any longer; it is all meaningless. Fornication is a burden and love is impossible. And yet, what is it about? How to account for the flight, the coldness, the refusal? We have Querry's "aridity" seen by the priests at the leper colony, but we do not have the love affairs or the life of the great architect that make the extraordinary final emptiness important. We see the soul at a point of theological instability, and there only.

Greene has a unique gift for plot and a miraculous way of finding a clever objective correlative for his spiritual perplexities. Loss of faith in art and love equals the "cure" of the leper, mutilated, but at last without pain. The humid tropical atmosphere, the tsetse flies, the intense *colons,* with their apologies and their arrogance, the strained, disputatious priests, interestingly pockmarked with weaknesses: this is the properly exotic and threatening setting for the Greene dialogue. *The Burnt-Out Case* seemed a partial failure to

V. S. Pritchett in his *New Statesman* review. He felt the influence of the stage had been unfortunate and worked less well than an earlier absorption of film technique. Yet he is not entirely dissatisfied and decides that Querry, the hero, succeeds as a vehicle for certain ideas if not as a "man." Pritchett calls Graham Greene, "the most piercing and important of our novelists now."

Frank Kermode in a brilliant article in *Encounter* is unhappy about *The Burnt-Out Case*. He finds it "so far below one's expectation that the questions arise, was the expectation reasonable and has there been any previous indication that a failure of this kind was a possibility?" In Kermode's view *The End of the Affair* is Greene's best novel because, to simplify, here the author more openly and with greater seriousness faces his case against God.

Querry, a builder of Catholic churches, is only, the novel tells us, "a legal Catholic." He doesn't pray, he loathes being dragged into other people's lives by the ropes of his religion and his fame; he doesn't want his sins to be made interesting as priests in novels like to do with villains; he resents having his vices stubbornly interpreted as incipient virtues. Father Thomas frantically insists upon accepting Querry's devastated spirit. "Don't you see that you've been given the grace of aridity? Perhaps even now you are walking in the footsteps of St. John of the Cross, the *noche oscura*." In trying to come to some sort of judgment about Greene as a novelist one would have to ask himself whether a significant picture of modern life in the last thirty years could be made from doctrinal puzzles, seminarian wit and paradox, private jokes, Roman Catholic exclusiveness. The characters take their sexual guilt and stand at the edge of damnation discussing possibilities for fresh theological interpretations. They are weary and romantic and fascinated by suffering and they look upon themselves and their feelings in a peculiarly intense Catholic-convert way, a sort of intellectual, clannish, delighted sectarianism. The question is not, in the great Russian manner, how one can live without God, or with God; the question is how one can exist as a moral, or immoral, man without running into vexing complications with the local priest. Marriage, love, sex, pride, art, no matter where you turn things are not quite as the Church would have it and to function at all one has to break rules or offer new versions of the old.

Of course Greene is fascinated by sin and heresy; it could not be otherwise. His terse novels, with their clear, firm themes and symbolic situations, are acted out by men with beautifully apt gifts for language, men raised on Cardinal Newman and Ronald Knox. His world is anti-psychological; the world of psychoanalytical motivation does not exist; its questions are never raised, its interpretations never suggested. Class, childhood, history are irrelevant, too. These are indeed peculiar novels. The omission of so much life and meaning, of the drama of social and psychological existence would seem to be ultimately limiting. There is a sense of disfiguration, baffling sometimes, and yet always intellectually exciting. Everything is sharper and more brilliant than the effects of other writers. God is a sort of sub-plot and the capricious way He treats Roman Catholics is a suspenseful background to love and boredom and pity. It is most perplexing.

How often Greene sees the living thing as a dead or trivial object, an article of manufacture. "A smile like a licorice stick"; "the pouches under his eyes were like purses that contained the smuggled memories of a disappointing life"; "he was like the kind of plant people put in bathrooms, reared on humidity, shooting too high. He had a small black moustache like a smear of city soot and his face was narrow and flat and endless, like an illustration of the law that two parallel lines never meet."

Licorice sticks, purses filled with snakes, leggy bathroom plants are lined up for the argument, the great debate over a whisky and soda at some peaceful, intellectual Priory. And meanwhile it is really to church that Sarah (*The End of the Affair*) is going and not to meet her lover. God laughs maliciously. On this stage, with its oddly clear and yet humanly peculiar themes, with its weary, engaging purity of design, these brilliant, original works take place, each one as arresting as the other, Catholic-convert dramas of sex and renunciation, belief and defiance.

1961

9 / America and Dylan Thomas

He died, grotesquely like Valentino, with mysterious, weeping women at his bedside. His last months, his final agonies, his utterly woeful end were a sordid and spectacular drama of broken hearts, angry wives, irritable doctors, frantic bystanders, rumors and misunderstandings, neglect and murderous permissiveness. The people near him visited indignities upon themselves, upon him, upon others. There seems to have been a certain amount of competition at the bedside, assertions of obscure priority. The honors were more and more vague, confused by the ghastly, suffering needs of this broken host and by his final impersonality. No one seems to have felt his wife and children had any divine rights but that they, too, had each day to earn their place on the open market in the appalling contest of Thomas's last years. Could it have happened quite this way in England? Were his last years there quite as frenzied and unhealthy as his journeys to America? He was one of ours, in a way, and he came back here to die with a terrible and fabulous rightness. (Not ours, of course, in his talents, his work, his joys, but ours in his sufferings, his longings, his demands.) "Severe alcoholic insult to the brain," the doctors said.

Dylan Thomas was loved and respected abroad, but he

was literally *adored* in America. Adored, too, with a queer note of fantasy, with a baffled extravagance that went beyond his superb accomplishments as a poet, his wit, amazing and delightful at all times, his immense abilities on the public platform. He was first-rate: one need not be ashamed to serve him or to pursue him. He was also, and perhaps this was more important to some of his admirers, doomed, damned, whatever you will, undeniably suffering and living in the extremest reaches of experience. As Eliot observed about Byron: after the theatricalism, the posing, the scandals, you had to come back to the fact that Byron was, nevertheless, genuinely disreputable. And so it was with Thomas. Behind his drinking, his bad behavior, his infidelities, his outrageousness, there was always his real doom. His condition was clearly critical. It couldn't go on much longer.

There was a certain element of drama in Thomas's readings that had nothing to do with his extraordinary powers. His story preceded him wherever he went; the perverse publicity somehow reached every town before he did and so the drama of his visit started before he arrived. Would he, first of all, really make it? (Awful if he didn't, with the tickets sold, hall hired, cocktail canapes made in advance.) Would he arrive only to break down on the stage? Would some dismaying scene take place at the faculty party? Would he be offensive, violent, obscene? These were alarming and yet exciting possibilities. Here, at last, was a poet in the grand, romantic style, a wild and inspired spirit not built for comfortable ways. He could be allowed anything. They would give him more drinks when he was dying of drink; they would let him spit in the eternal eye of the eternal head of the department, pinch the eternal faculty wife, insult the dull, the ambitious, the rich, tell obscene stories, use four-letter words. It did not make any difference. Thomas was acknowledged, unconsciously perhaps, to be beyond judgment, to be already living a tragic biography, nearing some certain fatality.

And he could make all the passes he chose, have all the love affairs, since the unspoken admission always was that he was doomed, profoundly ill, living as a character in a book, and his true love, beyond all others at this time, was alcohol. Yet so powerful and beguiling was his image—the image of a self-destroying, dying young poet of genius—that he aroused the most sacrificial longings in women. He had lost his looks, he was disorganized to a degree beyond belief, he had a wife and children in genuine need, and yet young ladies *felt* they had fallen in love with him. They fought over him; they nursed him while he retched and suffered and had delirium; they stayed up all night with him and yet went to their jobs the next morning. One girl bought cowboy suits for his children. Enormous mental, moral and physical adjustments were necessary to those who would be the companions of this restless, frantic man. The girls were up to it—it was not a hardship, but a privilege.

Apparently no one felt envious of Thomas or bitter about the attention he received. Even here he was an interesting exception. The explanation for the generosity lay first of all in the beauty and importance of his verse: this circumstance was the plain ground from which the elaborate and peculiar flowering of Thomas's American experience sprang. The madness of the infatuated is, after all, just an exaggeration of the reasonable assent of the discriminating. And so Thomas's personal greatness began it all, and the urgency of his drinking, his uncontrollable destructiveness seemed to add what was needed beyond his talents. He was both a success and a failure in a way we find particularly appealing. What he represented in the vividness of his success and failure was real and of irresistible power to certain art-conscious Americans. He had everything and "threw it all away." In him sophisticated schoolteachers, bright young girls, restless wives, bohemians, patrons and patronesses, found a poet they could love. He was not conservative, not snobbish, not middle-class, not alarmingly intellectual; he was a wild genius who needed caring for. And he was in a pattern we can recognize all too easily—the charming young man of great gifts, willfully going down to ruin. He was Hart Crane, Poe, F. Scott Fitzgerald, the stuff of which history is made, and also, unexpectedly, something of a great actor; indeed he was actually a great actor in a time when the literary style runs to the scholarly and the clerical. He satisfied a longing for the extreme. He was incorrigible and you never knew what he might do. He was fantastically picturesque. His Anglo-Welsh accent delighted everyone who heard it. Every college girl had her Dylan Thomas anecdote and it was usually scandalous, since he had a pronounced gift for that. His fees were exceeded only by the Sitwells, *tous les deux,* and by Eliot. His drinking had made him, at least superficially, as available as a man running for office. Everyone knew him, heard him, drank with him, nursed him. He was both immoderately available and, in the deepest sense, utterly unavailable too. His extraordinary gregariousness was a sign of his extremity. He knew everyone in the world, but for a long time he had perhaps been unable to know anyone. Oddly enough, at the end Thomas was more "fashionable" than he had ever been in his happier days. Even excess, carried off with so great a degree of authenticity and compulsiveness, has a kind of *chic.*

John Malcolm Brinnin's book, *Dylan Thomas in America,* has been praised by some critics, but many others have felt a good deal of moral annoyance about the work. They have found Brinnin a false friend, and they have decided his material might better have gone unpublished. Yet, it seems unfair to accuse Brinnin of treachery or of commercial exploitation of his friendship with Thomas—the most astonishing aspect of his record is just the wild and limitless nature of his devotion to his subject. It has, at times, almost the character of an hallucination.

"The sharpest scrutiny is the condition of enduring fame," Froude said as he set out to tell all he knew about Carlyle. This is the dominion of history and scholarship. But Brinnin's book does not seem to be a product of the historical impulse as we usually think of it. His journal is truly an obsessive document and is most unusual for that reason. It is not easy to think of anything else quite like it, anything one might justly compare it with. His commitment to his subject is of such an overwhelming degree that he cannot leave out anything. He treats Dylan Thomas as a great force of nature and would no more omit an infidelity or a hang-over than a weatherman would suppress the news of an ugly storm. In certain respects, the book is not a piece of composition at all, but is rather the living moment with its repetitions, its naïveté, its peculiar acceptance of and compulsive attachment to every detail of Thomas's sad existence. It is as flat and true as a calendar. As a record, it is oddly open and marked by a helpless, uncomfortable fascination on Brinnin's part. For him Thomas was an addiction. Having once taken on the friendship, Brinnin was trapped, spell-bound, enlisted in a peculiar mission. Here are sentences from the early pages of the journal which tell of Thomas's first American visit: "He slept, breathing heavily, as I fingered through some English magazines he had brought with him, and watched the early lights of Manhattan come on through the sleet. As I contemplated Dylan's deep sleep,

I tried first to comprehend and then to accept the quality (it was too early to know the dimensions) of my assignment . . . no one term would serve to define a relationship which had overwhelmed my expectations and already forced upon me a personal concern that was constantly puzzled, increasingly solicitous and, I knew well by now, impossible to escape."

Although Brinnin was the business agent for Thomas's American performances, his presence is due, not to business concerns, but to the notion of a mysterious and compelling destiny, a fatigued and yet somehow compulsory attendance. The "too late now to turn back" theme is heard again and again. "I knew that, above all now, I wanted to take care of him. . . . Just as certainly, I knew that I wanted to get rid of him, to save myself from having to be party to his self-devouring miseries and to forestall any further waiting upon his inevitable collapses." Reading such passages, you are reminded of the fatal commitments in Poe's work, of those nightmares of the irresistible and irrational involvement. Even Thomas's first visit was anticipated by Brinnin as a gloomy necessity; he approached the arrival with a painful and helpless alarm, and yet with a feeling of the inevitable. The commitment was of a quality impossible to analyze. It went beyond any joy that might or might not be found in Thomas's company, beyond mutual interests and personal affinity. It was so deep and so compelling that despair was its natural mood. Because of the fabulous difficulty of Thomas's character, this mood of despair seems more appropriate than the carousing, robust tone some others fall into when they talk of Thomas. In Brinnin's book it is always, in feeling at least, the dead, anguished middle of a drunken night. The despair, the wonder and the helplessness start the book and lead up to the grim, apoplectic end. There is no pretense that it was fun. It was maddening, exhausting, but there it was. And after Thomas died there was no release from the strain because the book had to be written, fulfilled with the same dogged, tired fascination the author felt in the case of the actual events. The self-effacement of the style seems a carry-over from the manner one adopts when he sits, sober, exhausted and anxious, with a drunken friend whose outbursts and ravings one is afraid of. The lists of guests at a party, the lecture dates, the financial details—the reader takes these in nervously, flatly, with the sense of a strange duty being honored. The girls, the quarrels, the summers and winters, the retchings, the humiliations, the heights and the depths—they are all presented in the same gray, aching tone. The writing of the book seems to have been the same sort of hallucinated task as the planning of the lecture tours. There is a unique concentration upon the elemental, upon how much Thomas slept, how much he could be made to eat, upon the momentary predicaments. Of character analysis or literary analysis, there is very little. This is the terrifying breath of life, but of a life without words. "He was ill and downcast again in the morning. . . ." "We broke our trip to Connecticut by a stop in Sturbridge, to drink ale before the wood-burning fireplace of an old inn, and arrived at the University just in time to spend an informal hour with the fourteen students of my graduate seminar." To spend *an hour* with the *fourteen* students! One does not know what to make of the inclusion of so much fact and figure. Thomas's conversation, so rare and beautiful, is not captured at all. The record is of another kind. It is certainly bemused and depressed and yet it is outlandishly successful as a picture of the prosaic circumstances of some months in a dramatic life.

Near the end: "There he ate an enormous dinner—a dinner which, in the course of events, was to be his last full meal." Dylan Thomas died in St. Vincent's Hospital in New York City. His death was miserable and before he passed into the final coma he had delirium tremens, horrors, agonies, desire for death, and nearly every physical and mental pain one can imagine. Brinnin does not try to render the great denouement, but again it is, in an odd and indefinable fashion, rendered by the dazed and peculiarly accurate and endless detail. "His face was wan and expressionless, his eyes half-opening for moments at a time, his body inert." The actual death: "Dylan was pale and blue, his eyes no longer blindly searching but calm, shut, and ineffably at peace. When I took his feet in my hand all warmth was gone. . . ." The final line of the record does fly upward in intention, but it is more clumsy, more earthbound than all of the repetitive detail of all the thousands of preceding lines and it does not even seem true. "Now, as always, where Dylan was, there were no tears at all."

Could it have happened quite this way in England? It is an unhappy circumstance for us that Thomas should have died here, far from his family, far from the scenes he had lived in and written about. The maniacal permissiveness and submissiveness of American friends might, for all we know, have actually shortened Thomas's life, although he was ill and driven in England too. But there was a certain amount of poison in our good will. In the acceptance of his tragic condition there was a good deal of indifference and self-deception. The puzzling contentiousness of his friends and the ugly competition for his favors remain coldly in our minds. According to Brinnin, Thomas made these frantic flights to America because of his "conviction that his creative powers were failing, that his great work was finished." He feared he was "without the creative resources to maintain and expand his position." The financial benefit was destroyed by the familiar condition of our economic life: he spent every penny he made just as soon as he had it in his hands. His wife and his mother wanted him to stay at home *in order* to earn a living for his family. Furthermore Caitlin Thomas felt he had been "spoiled" in America, that he came here for "flattery, idleness and infidelity." Perhaps one shouldn't read too much between the lines, but it is hard not to get the idea that Thomas's American friends, with a cynical show of piety, treated these accusations and feelings as outrageous. They, sinking sensuously into their own suspicious pity, flattered and allowed and encouraged right to the brink of the grave.

In England we have Brinnin's own observation that the deference shown to Thomas was of a quieter, less unreal and unbalancing sort. It might almost have passed for a lack of interest. In a London pub with Thomas, Brinnin was impressed that the poet was, for once, "not the object of everyone's attention." Here in America the approbation was extreme, the notice sometimes hysterical, the pace killing. The cost of these trips was "disproportionate to the rewards." The trip before the last one was felt to be "too exhausting to contemplate," and still it was not only contemplated, it was arranged, it happened, and was followed by an unbelievable another, the last of the three. In these tours Thomas seems like nothing so much as a man in the films, addressing the audience cheerfully, but with a gun in his back. It was a ghastly affair, preserved faithfully and grimly by Brinnin. There is an element in this story of ritual and fantasy, a phantasmagoria of pain and splendor, of talent and untimely death. And there is something else: the sober and dreary fact of the decline of our literary life, its thinness and fatigue. From this Thomas was, to many, a brief reprieve.

1956

David Riesman's collection of essays, *Individualism Reconsidered*, establishes this writer as a novel fact, a kind of invention whose value may be uncertain but whose conspicuous existence has to be faced. Riesman has come upon the
scene like the bubble house, television, cinemascope; that is
to say he has been a possibility for some years but was not
actually on the market until fairly recently. Expected,
needed, he stepped forth all smiles to meet the call. His role
is difficult to name—is he a teacher, psychologist, sociologist,
historian, philosopher? But that does not mean it is easy to
escape his notions and effect. A traveler returned from afar
might well, for a quick readjustment to the local intellectual
life, read *The Lonely Crowd* in a hurry and set aside the
latest works of literature for his leisure.

Moderate, energetic, as he is, Riesman's originality is to
have chosen the utter present. His sheer contemporaneity,
his briskly marching in the forward ranks—by comparison
with this, many a younger man appears a bit sallow and
run-down by the world of comics, television, pop tunes,
"crazy" teen-agers, all the raw diet Riesman thrives upon.
His fate is this present postwar decade of prosperity; the

two suit each other; the man, we feel, has been waiting around for the time. There is often here, as in the Eisenhower government, the atmosphere of a new administration after twenty years of reform, lamentation and national doubt.

But struck as one is by the timeliness of Riesman's references, there is also a perplexing sadness about him. He is a cheerfully curious and lively observer, as free of "liberal piety" as one of the teen-agers he is so much interested in; yet he has his secret sharer, a tortured image hidden below the deck, the outcast (or rather the *outmoded* in Riesman's case) whose claims make even this bustling man uncomfortably itchy. Riesman is, for that reason, a somewhat nervous and uncertain thinker. There is a great deal in his works of "however" and "nevertheless" and "on the other hand it must be remembered"—expressions of honorable uneasiness, a generous measure of propitiation. Invariably after an exhortation in one direction, we are reminded of the great value mankind has found in taking the opposite path. Trailing this mind so soundly opinionated and expressive on the whole, you wonder about those vigilant glances into the enemy corner, the tense alertness that wants to startle and pacify at the same time. Perhaps the trouble is that Riesman is going with too young a crowd; he is forty-five and never likely to be whole-heartedly happy in the company of youth and confidence, even though this youthful, consuming, money-free time we live in is his interesting destiny.

In addition to the chronological displacement which makes Riesman's thought sometimes puzzling, he is confusing because of his quite singular need to be effective in the most simple meaning of the term. He likes to select his "truth" according to the occasion, obeying in this odd way the law of supply and demand. Like a therapist whose duty is to persuade and guide, now he tries this line and then another, following the patient's moods. "But it is not enough to know the audience; one must also know *their* context. They may be so buffeted by their adversaries that they need, at least temporarily, to have their prejudices confirmed rather than shaken. For instance, girl students at some of our liberal universities need occasionally to be told that they are not utterly damned if they discover within themselves anti-Negro or anti-Semitic reactions—else they may expiate their guilt by trying to solve the race question in marriage." Riesman's desire to lead back to the barn that rare, mulish girl bent upon a *mésalliance* seems a little over-anxious. What parents, friends, relatives, society, expediency insist upon in such urgent terms need not be taken upon himself by a busy sociologist.

"What may on the surface appear to me as my courageous choice of an unorthodox and unpopular position may turn out on closer examination to be a form of exhibitionism. Or I may be more conciliatory than is warranted because I want to be liked." It is hard to know how to judge a thinker whose intellectual positions are so profoundly modified by "psychology," who treats his own opinions as if they were those of a character in a novel he was writing. Or again, standing in the center of the stage, watching the audience assemble, he waits for the feel of the thing and then chooses his rubbery mask, comic one way, tragic upside down. Solid success, effective therapy, animated delivery—all of this is achieved, but frequently at the expense of some of the brilliance that undoubtedly might be there otherwise. Riesman has genuine vitality and, of course, remarkable gifts. But if you make yourself honey the flies will eat you.

Inner-direction and other-direction: these categories made popular by Riesman's writing correspond very neatly to the character structures described by Erich Fromm. Other-direction is held to be typical of our present age; this phenomenon is very much the same as Fromm's "marketing orientation." In Riesman's work the inner-directed society "develops in its typical members a social character whose conformity is insured by their tendency to acquire early in life an internalized set of goals." The person usual in such a society has "certain general aims and drives—the drive to work hard, save money, or to strive for rectitude or for fame . . . as against the other-directed person who grows up in a much more amorphous social system, where alternate destinations cannot be clearly chosen at an early age."

The other-directed person shows "a tendency to be sensitized to the expectations and preferences of others." A detail of his psychic existence: "The feeling of powerlessness of the other-directed character is, then, the result in part of the lack of genuine commitment to work. . . . From this it follows that the other-directed person is not able to judge the work of others. . . ." Neither the other-directed nor the inner-directed designation is meant to be a value judgment in the strictest sense; however, Riesman does introduce a desirable direction, the "autonomous" person (Fromm's "productive" person). This person has the courage and strength to act out his destiny and character with responsibility and confidence. No one will be found to dispute the excellence of such citizens.

In describing his various character structures Riesman is extraordinarily imaginative and even amusing. His "other-directed" products of progressive education, restless, homeless, precariously in the know, are like those bug-eyed dreams pouring out of a space ship. These "others" come equipped with "radar" which tells them what the gang is thinking; the "inners" have a "gyroscope" to keep them on the path of duty. The others zoom about in an abundance economy with a declining population; the inners battled with scarcity. Others have a diffused anxiety; inners suffer from guilt and shame when they fall below their own standards. The inners expect to have to master their environment; the others are concerned with mastering and presenting themselves as a commodity, competing with other personalities. And so it goes, rather like those old tests in psychology class in which the spirit was unmasked in the squeezing of a tube of tooth paste.

Just what contribution this sort of inquiry makes one cannot be sure. There is reason to suspect readers enjoy the display of "types" as they would a new pastime. One can combine new classifications with old ones by other investigators and create a fascinating game of Who Am I? The trouble is, of course, that in the final summation the type-maker is always obliged to admit that most people are a combination of types and so the fun is somewhat reduced by yet another admission that even a single human being can hardly ever be clearly placed. Riesman has his "varieties" of inner- and other-direction and Fromm his "blends."

Historically, it may be true that other-direction is more typical of the present time than of the past. However, it is certainly not new, as the literature of the past shows. For every person with inherited ideals and driving will there was another—fluid, adaptable, painfully attuned to others, terrified that the cut of his waistcoat would not be quite the thing worn by fashionable young men in London, fearful of exhibiting a failure of "inside dopesterism." Among contemporary Americans it is true that many are "tense and anxious lest their radar not bring them the latest bulletins," but there is still quite a lot of secret inner-direction. Many a Madison Avenue advertising executive has worked, struggled and endured; his rise upward has been as bitter, silent and sternly pursued as that of an old robber baron.

The Lonely Crowd is the most popular and readable of Riesman's works. Its success rests upon a solid basis of cleverness, up-to-dateness, knowingness and humor. Riesman writes about the shift from "bringing up children to bringing up father." He knows the supermarket, *The Joy of Cooking*, the "sincerity" of Frank Sinatra's style, a magazine called *Hot Rod*. He flatters and consoles us by sharing our own secret acquaintance with the "media" and even encourages one in the investigation of these pleasures, going so far as to state that those parents who are frightened of TV and the comics are really jealous of their children's expert knowledge of them. (This amazing notion is something like saying a fat man despairs of ever understanding a child's love for a candy bar.) Just as Riesman forgives one for his vices, he at the same time admits one into a more exclusive realm by using as examples "The Other Margaret" by Lionel Trilling, articles by Mary McCarthy, along with the classical works of sociology and economics.

There are times when Riesman's style in *The Lonely Crowd* is a bit *too* worldly, reminding one suddenly of the gags of radio comics. An example of this is the phrase "chimney-corner media" as a description of folk-tale entertainments of "tradition-directed" societies. But on the whole *The Lonely Crowd* is his best book and better in the short than in the longer version because of this writer's tendency to repetition.

Faces in the Crowd is a long, rather dull series of "portraits," meant to give concrete examples of Riesman's character types. This work is a "project"—expensive, pretentious, dubious. Questionnaires, interviews, interpretations, all of this decoration in the end succeeds in giving us merely a superficial psychoanalytical report on some elected persons. (The only genuine reward of these heavy pages is a fantast named Henry Friend. Friend is fifteen years old, goes to a progressive school in Los Angeles, is being analyzed by a Reichian and at the time of the interview was the founder of his local Young Citizens for Wallace Club.) The interpretations are offered with quite a bit of authority and relish, but nevertheless the dangers of triviality and pointlessness loom up on every page. For instance, there is the following comment upon a young "subject" who greatly admires the work of Thomas Mann: "I am struck, moreover, by a certain surprising provinciality in the judgments themselves; Mann has little standing with the avant-garde, German or American, but only with middlebrows." This shows what a din of static comes to one who listens with too eager an ear to the buzz of some imaginary goddess of Fashion.

It seems likely that Riesman's projects and interpretations are much more vivid than those one may expect from other sociologists. Indeed the mind sinks into despair at the thought of the other projects mentioned in this book: the Cornell group trying to define persons who possess "social creativity"; a Brooklyn College group interviewing "self-actualizing" individuals. These scholars, defiantly gay and busy, are mad lovers of the moon—moonstruck, they follow the course of a smile, trace the path of a sigh.

Freud and Veblen: Riesman is uncomfortably challenged by these figures. Great they are, strange and wonderful, and yet a little unreal somehow, a bit *impossible* with so much "askew" in their "character structures," with their sudden explosions of mischief and selfishness. They are cocky, intransigent, insistent; they threaten the young with their resistance to compromise, their unsuitability, like that of a brilliant but unstable suitor one must reject for our present-day America, a land dizzy with jobs and goods and "mobile" personalities, heroically consuming on the world's material and spiritual market.

The general impression one gets from Riesman's book on Veblen is that Veblen was tiresomely simple. A brilliant goof who didn't care about clothes and wanted to prevent other people from enjoying them. He built himself a log cabin in the woods; he was "provincial," not sure of himself and therefore filled with the need to exaggerate and insist upon his difference. ". . . When we think how much suffering he underwent and caused, we cannot unequivocally condemn the propaganda of adjustment to which contemporary eccentrics are exposed." The disenchantment of Veblen and that of Mark Twain is somehow not of the first order; these Middle Westerners are not secure enough socially to afford the "ennui-pessimism of the Eastern patricians," such as Henry and Brooks Adams. In Veblen's character we are told there is a great deal of the "saboteur"—he is always sneaking about, slyly refusing to co-operate. "His strategies of non-compliance are in this interpretation only the end product, codified by recognition, of a repressed inner urge to show off." And "more important was Veblen's fear of eminence, of the dark unnameable dangers attendant upon putting oneself forward, out in the open, an object of critical notice, a target before spectators." But this is fantastic—Veblen *was* great and many a man ready to stand up and be counted among the eminent is not.

Riesman suggests that the desire to provoke envy, the psychological basis of Veblen's "conspicuous consumption," has in prosperous America been replaced by the *fear* of being envied. This notion is impossible to credit; the fear of being envied is an eccentricity, just as outrageous to the majority as it has always been. The desire to repudiate their privileges does exist for certain people and is nothing new. The princess and the footman is not so different from the "liberal girl" in her occasional excursions into the lower orders. One of the pleasant rights of those on top is to sink, whereas the lowly have only the possibility of trying laboriously to move upward.

The essays on Freud in *Individualism Reconsidered* are very striking and often more than a little puzzling. Freud is immense, yes, but is this striving, gloomy thinker "right" for us, for America? Riesman, smiling loftily at "pessimism" as if it were an old contraption now replaced by a new manufacture, often finds our American experience to be mysteriously different from the generally human one. Freud could not foresee what would happen to our economy and so he is a bit out of date—an attitude that reminds one of other critics' frantic assertion that Freud could not say much to us because his clinical knowledge came largely from wealthy Viennese Jews. The struggle for life, the brutal need to make one's bread and one's fate in a competitive society were taken for granted by Freud. Bitterly enduring and striving, he did not foresee an America in which hunger is confined to people on a reducing diet. Riesman says about Freud, "Certainly, his utilitarian and Philistine attitudes toward work and play were both central to his own view of life and a dominant note in his cultural environment. But what really matters to us is that by virtue of his greatness—

by virtue, too, of the fact that he was on the whole a liberator of men—Freud has succeeded in imposing on a later generation a mortgage of reactionary and constricting ideas that were by no means universally held even in his own epoch." (The difficulty of extracting the meat from claws like that is one of the experiences of Riesman's writing on Freud.) Freud came from a job-minded society. His ideas "circulate today in an American society that has much more chance to be leisure-minded and play-minded." Let us hope Riesman has not mistaken a footnote for the main text, since any important economic constriction would seriously confound nearly all of his impressions.

In another instance Riesman professes himself amazed at Freud's desire to get on in the world. "While he was apt to minimize the extent of his own ambition, it did not trouble him to avow his wish to be a full professor, to be famous, to be an 'authority' . . . ." Freud also was rather embarrassing, in this view, in his gratitude for worldly honors, for the invitation to speak at Clark University, in speaking of the Goethe Prize given to him by the City of Frankfort as "the climax of my life." Psychoanalyzing these sentiments, Riesman says, "here again one is confronted with the problem of Freud's ambivalence toward authority. . . . In spite of himself, Freud could not help his preoccupation with questions of rank within the institutions of solid-seeming Vienna and, beyond Vienna, solid-seeming 'official' German science and chauvinistically hostile but culturally reputed Parisian science." No matter what Freud "could not help," Riesman's grandeur dazzles us in this instance.

Other interesting notions on Freud: "Freud's work, as I read his own account of it, seems to me of the very greatest intellectual interest; beside such detective work, even that of Sherlock Holmes is pallid and limited." This bizarre comparison is one a man might ponder for a day without learning how it was arrived at or what the "even" means; a mysterious image, like something one has in his mind at the end of a troubled dream. Still this is not nearly so original as Riesman's idea that Freud "patronizes" childhood; this conclusion is drawn from the fact that Freud thought children did not want to grow up and had to be forced to do so by parents and society, by pain and disappointment.

Both Veblen and Freud are scolded by this author because of their lack of "sophistication." Sophistication stands enthroned in Riesman's mind, that indefinable something— nature's noblemen like Freud and Veblen may have their genius but this appealing quality is not theirs. Veblen's queerness is something of a pose, a temper tantrum, the clever peasant's way of clogging up the works; Freud's gloom is cold mutton from old Vienna. In the end it is all well. After his lengthy animadversions, Riesman redeems his men with a flourish. "In fact, it is just Veblen's irreverence we stand in need of in a day when total commitment is being asked of everyone." And Freud: "Having made these criticisms of Freud's view of religion, I think we must grant his tremendous contribution to our understanding of it." The ship rocks, one is vaguely distressed, but the forward course is maintained.

Individualism Reconsidered is certainly an impressive volume, thirty essays, many of considerable length and concerned with a large number of subjects. Still, the work has very often a peculiar glassy brightness that leaves us in a mood of discomfort. There are many awkwardly written passages that remind one all too readily of sociology books:

"Athletic prowess may be declining as an unequivocal assurance of status, and certainly no other prowess can substitute for interpersonal competence as a guarantor of social success." High culture is sometimes recommended in jazzy tones, like an effective singing commercial. Those who read books are called "hard-cover men" and are to be distinguished from their soft, light-reading brothers. "Yet it is precisely on the good-sized, hard-cover book that the bookworm is nourished. He cannot bury himself in a moving image. . . . He is a creature who needs wide margins. For he tries to create amid all the pressures of contemporary culture a kind of 'social space' around himself, an area of privacy. He does this by tieing himself in his thinking and feeling to sources of some relative permanence—hence impersonal—while remaining somewhat impermeable to the fluctuating tastes, panics, and most menacing of all, the appeals to be 'adjusted' from his contemporaries."

From such thoughts and from the title of the book, one is urged to conclude that Riesman is on the side of "individualism." And yet it is a "variety" of individualism and not the pure thing we are used to. Its most personal note is not the appeal for culture or "autonomy" but the part of Riesman that most yearns for complete acceptance of our world, for a good opinion of ourselves, an admission of well-being. This is reasonable therapy, but it may not pass as history or philosophy.

Muckrakers, reformers, expatriates, pessimists, sectarians—Riesman dreads these as a star dreads a meeting with a has-been. This writer is not so much a conservative as an optimist: he wants to enjoy the present, he looks for the violet between the rocks. Sometimes his optimism mounts up to a harmless but unnerving mania, as in the comparison of the move to the suburbs with the exploration and settlement of the frontier. "But frontier towns are not usually very attractive. And frontier behavior is awkward: people have not yet learned to behave comfortably in the new surroundings." The pioneer woman is recognized by the touch of oregano she puts in the casserole. "Among men particularly, the demand that one must enjoy food, and not simply stow it away, is relatively new, and again these pioneers are awkwardly self-conscious."

These cool-eyed scouts tracking the forests of Suburbia, moving on to new "frontiers of consumption" are no doubt singing to the accompaniment of an electric guitar during the long, lonesome evenings.

"Some Observations on Intellectual Freedom," which Riesman published in 1953, is his most extravagant and lover-like address to our present situation. (True, there is an enormous eye winking over the reader's head. In a later postscript Riesman more or less repudiates the main text.) Answering an article in which Archibald MacLeish expressed certain fears for the freedom of the intellectual in America, Riesman takes a passionate stand against such unhealthy imaginings. ". . . The naming of evils, intended as a magical warding-off, can have the opposite effect." By taking a positive attitude, looking for the best, Riesman hopes to comfort and reshape the diseased extremity like a corrective shoe. MacLeish was disturbed by a growing disrespect for the intellectual, but Riesman thinks: "In a way, the attention that the intellectuals are getting these days, though much of it is venomous and indecent, testifies to the great improvement in our status over that of an earlier day. What might not Henry Adams have given for such signs of recognition!"

There is some of the cheerful impudence here of a press

agent who thinks his client's arrest is better than nothing.
. . . That were some love, but little policy.

1954

Postscript 1961:

Our prosperous, unique, odd society was wild, we felt,
but splendid, too, like a run-away horse. Right after the war,
the therapy for all our moral discomforts was a daily recital
of the sins of Communism and the Soviet Union and the
subsequent healthy enjoyment of our own virtues, or at
least of our absent sins. Nothing much was asked of us
beyond that, no other sacrifice beyond reminding ourselves
how good we were as a people and a system and that we
did not need to suffer the infection of despairing self-criti-
cism. These easy days did not last long. How quickly we
showed an unexpected vulnerability, from within first—the
"quality of our prosperity"—and from without in the vexing
technological success of the Soviet Union. Our hopes seemed
to fall away. It was as if we had bought one of those brilliant
gardenia plants too soon before Easter and had watched the
rudely forced green buds, with the white petals tightly
curled inside, fall off one by one, without coming to bloom.

Sometimes one has the feeling of an almost supernatural
character to the shifts and changes in our national mood.
They appear beyond the prose of cause and effect; to live
through them is to know the ineffable pain and fascination
of tragedy. It was such a short, short time. We were all
ready, as a people, to go in for a monumental, historic
relaxation of soul and even of muscle, a relaxation of effort
that was truly new and whose ultimate meaning one could

not even guess at. Then, suddenly, in the blinking of an eye, we were asked to calculate how many millions we could lose and still "survive."

Our happier days had been described, with great cleverness and zest, and in the properly complicated, ambiguous manner by David Riesman, particularly in *The Lonely Crowd.* He had, or so it seemed, made the sort of adjustment that allowed him to accept much that others shrank from assimilating. Riesman saw everything dangerous, but he did not take the defects of our society with too great a seriousness. He was, rather, often amused by them and the reader of his books was somehow invited to get with it, too.

I remember a windy night last spring and the small group of people gathered in midtown Manhattan for a meeting of the Committee for Cultural Freedom. (I hope it is not unfair to remember this occasion and the mood of it. The opinions expressed were not—or so I believe—secret ones; in fact, the declarations were urgent and passionate.) Diana Trilling, with great energy of mind and at considerable length, urged upon the group the demonic theory of Communism and the Soviet Union and further seemed to insist that the debate about our national destiny, in so far as Russia was concerned, should remain static, a contest between good and evil. She seemed to have found, back in time, the meaning of the struggle and to consider it settled, as if it were some issue of past history and all the research had been done. Nuclear war played no special part in her vivid picture. What she feared was the inner weakening of the intellectual's will to resist, a weakening due to the cold war, the need for negotiation, the necessity—at least as some saw it—for co-existence.

I bring this matter up because David Riesman played a part; he was a sort of absent ghost, floating in and out of

the argument, threatening Mrs. Trilling's religious view of
the political subject. Many other minds might threaten her
vision in this detail, but it was dramatic to find Riesman
prominently and urgently doing so in his current writings.
It was most unexpected because he had in the past been
impatient with radical criticism and fear, and even scornful
at times of intransigence or utopian vision. But now—
ah, perfido! In an article in *Commentary* last year, Riesman (with Michael Maccoby) had written that the political
atmosphere in America was much less healthy than in
England. In England one could undertake "an active discussion . . . of alternatives to nuclear war, with the proposals
ranging from unilateral disarmament to diplomatic maneu-
vers aimed at easing particular points of tension in the cold
war, whether in China or in Germany." Riesman found our
ability to deal sensibly with the issue of Communism much
inferior to the British. "Even after the Klaus Fuchs case,
they [the British] in effect decided that they would rather
risk losing a few secrets to a few spies than turn the country
upside down in the alleged hope of flushing all enemy
agents out."

As I remember Mrs. Trilling's paper, she was particularly
disturbed by Riesman's psychological analysis, in the same
Commentary article, of the issue of "hard and soft anti-
communism." This phrase, or these phrases, are most unfortunate and of course contain almost infinite comic possibilities disconcerting to the normal discussion-group
atmosphere. The possibilities were not lost on the author of
The Lonely Crowd, even though he forbore to push them
too far. He noted that "American men seem constantly
pursued by the fear of unmanliness, and therefore feel the
need to present themselves as hard and realistic." The chief
point of Riesman's article and many of his recent political

writings was that he wished to change the debate about the cold war, which he saw not as a simple contest between America and Russia but as "the failure of a way of life." He took a radically critical position on the problem of Germany and on nuclear testing; he seemed almost a pacifist.

All of this was surprising from the man who had so much disliked, as Norman Birnhaum says, "the pretension of spiritual heroism," and who had reserved "an acerbity, uncommon for him, for those who do manifest a critical politics." Riesman had shown a suspiciously agile gift for accommodation to postwar America. One might ask oneself about the new pacifism, the desperate worry about nuclear war, the need to examine again the Soviet view on certain points—was all this just another quick shifting of the gears, another finger testing the wind? Perhaps the "hard anticommunists" would name it just that, but it would depend upon which direction you felt the wind to be coming from. It is hard to imagine popularity will follow such serious distaste for so many of our national attitudes.

The present activities of Riesman, his Pauline conversion, bear a relation to his work as a sociologist; they change his possibilities even more than he seems to realize. A new book, *Culture and Social Character,** points up the curious nature of his career. First of all, his very essence seems to contain a high degree of restlessness and vigilant self-examination and a natural tendency to revision. The mere idea of collecting essays about his work treats him as if he were a completed story, like, for instance, Max Weber. And, of course, it is not only that his professional career is far

* *Culture and Social Character:* The work of David Riesman reviewed, appraised and criticized by his contemporaries in Social Sciences. Edited by Seymour Lipset and Leo Lowenthal. The Free Press.

from finished, but that his past work is constantly being altered and revised and, because of the way he arrives at his opinions, being put out of order by history. Time, even a very short time, makes a great difference. For instance, there is a new preface to the paperback edition of *The Lonely Crowd*, a new preface to the paperback edition of his book on Veblen, a "reconsideration of *The Lonely Crowd*" (written along with his collaborator, Nathan Glazer), appended to this present collection of essays by his colleagues. Even all these second thoughts still do not give a sufficient idea of the actual changes in Riesman's position. In the preface to the new edition of *The Lonely Crowd* he explains some of his previous optimism in the following way: "We were writing at a time when the miasma that settled in the land during the era of the Cold War and the Eisenhower Administration was not yet at hand, complacency about America combined with anti-communism had not yet merged into the American Way." He admits "a too great readiness to consider traditional interpretations as 'dated.' " (A new name keeps appearing in Riesman's recent work, Reinhold Niebuhr and "tragic realism." I venture to guess, Riesman fashion, that this is for him the new thing.)

The rapid obsolescence of some of Riesman's observations came from his being too quick to turn observations into general statements. Fashions were mistaken for the enduring American character. Now, when the outside world seems to change more rapidly and more drastically than ever before, the amount of revision the busy opinionizer will be in for is too much to be practical. Even such a profound matter as the education of the young was changed, in the mind of important sections of our society, by the news of Sputnik and by that alone. New aspects of the national personality may be suddenly brought to light by a political or military event. For the sake of argument, one can imagine that if we were trapped and isolated behind a hard position from which we could not retreat, an America inner-directed in the manner of Dutch South Africa is a possibility. It is the overestimation of trends by Riesman that makes the use of the name of de Tocqueville misleading as a comparison.

To quote Norman Birnbaum again in his description of the changed Riesman: "The politics of abundance, in its American form, now strike him as less open; he is, in general, critical of America's role in the world. Most of all he is terribly frightened of the prospect of atomic war." The sociologists, in this collection, do not consider the possibility that a truly radical questioning of our life would make it impossible for Riesman to continue to use his old methods. The questionnaire and interview method of social research is particularly vulnerable, or so one would think. The interest in measuring vague details almost presupposes an acceptance of the central aims of the society. How could a man profoundly worried about the future of his country devote himself to what Riesman describes as "the enormous stream of social-psychological research now being devoted to conformity, yea-saying, acquiescence, etc. . . ." In a frightened nation, few will worry about what a small number of high school students think about success or excellence. This would be somewhat true even if we were not frightened, but the crisis makes these questionnaires unintelligible as an academic or professional pursuit. In this book the work of Elaine Sofer with college students is recommended for its creative way of approaching the measurement of inner-direction and other-direction. But the most striking thing about Miss Sofer's work is the trouble she has making anything meaningful out of the answers she got to her questions. The less pretentious public-opinion polls, concentrating on current, clear issues, are the most valid use of the method—and we all know how little use they are.

By all of this I mean to say that I was disappointed that the new Riesman did not, except in a few essays, particularly the one by Norman Birnbaum, appear in *Culture and Social Character*, and the appearance he does make in this book devoted to him is already partly out-of-date. His entrance into the political debate will make an enormous difference in his whole point of view. For the sociology he practiced in the past, the moment was everything, the eternity nothing. But the news of the day changes the attitudes these scholars are measuring faster than projects and books and scholarly papers can be brought out.

A word about the style of the sociologist, even though one hesitates to remark again on what has been so much spoken about—the barbarous language, the incoherence and ugliness of most of the writing. It took a great deal of will power on my part to read through this collection of essays. I suppose I shall be called one of those with a "grudge against sociology." And why not have a grudge? I have come to the belief that there is not merely an accidental relationship between bad writing and routine sociological research, but a wonderfully pure, integral relationship; the awkwardness is necessary and inevitable. The insights of these people will necessarily be "insightful," and speculation about "affection" will soon have you reading of the "high warmth factor" and "identification with the warmth indulger." It is the extreme fragility of the insights that leads to the debasement of language; the need to turn merely interesting and temporary observations into general theory and large application seems to be the source of the trouble with these incredible compositions. By seeking a false significance, a tone of professionalism, perhaps it is natural that the "affectionate person" will have to be called the "warmth indulger."

To return once more to Riesman, the rightness or even the permanence of his opinions cannot be decided now because there are so many remote conditions to be considered. However, it is always interesting to watch a man changing his mind, especially when the man has, like Riesman, had a huge success with his previous views. How can you describe such leaps into the discomforts of a critical position? Regret and courage seem to play equal parts—and from this meeting the most unusual possibilities suggest themselves.

Eugene O'Neill is certainly a very disturbing American figure. Perhaps no one of such desperate agonies and continuing success can be thought of as anything except a very special case. And yet there are ways in which he seems to have stepped into the despairing, muddy tracks already made by the suffering and disappointments of Poe and Melville. O'Neill's story is nearly incredible. His was a singularly distressing life and temperament. Almost any one around had an easier time. His art, in its defects and its power, did not have the sureness of the tradition out of which Poe and Melville came—it is only the alienation, the sense of melancholy fate that he shares with the earlier writers. O'Neill seems to have produced his work in unusual pain, because of his lack of the ordinary verbal gifts most important writers take for granted. One turns away from reading the new books* that have followed upon the success of his posthumous plays much puzzled, feeling here is the old story of misery and creation, but lived out in a special anguish and wonder and mystery.

* *O'Neill* by Arthur and Barbara Gelb; *The Tempering of Eugene O'Neill* by Doris Alexander; *O'Neill and his Plays,* edited by Oscar Cargill, N. Bryllion Fagin, William J. Fisher.

As a life, the O'Neill story unfolds like that most dismal and constricted of Russian family novels, *The Goloviev Family*. You feel the O'Neills are under a blight—or "curse," to use a more O'Neillish word. At every turn there is heartlessness and emotional deprivation and which is the cause, which the effect one cannot know. One tragedy after another—tragedies of excess, of self-destruction, of refusal and escape. And the foundation of all this, as we see it, was built upon the unusually successful talents of the father and the son.

Eugene O'Neill was the son of a popular actor, James O'Neill. *A Long Day's Journey into Night* gives the son's idea of his family, but, purely as biography, it is too much the chagrined son's view of his father and leaves out the cheerful, industrious and "lovable" side of the old actor as other people remembered him. Still, "other people" do not write the family story; it is always written from inside the prison, not from the street. The O'Neill children—Eugene and his brother, Jamie—were certainly exposed to the peculiar neglect that the very existence of a famous parent is so likely to create: the neglect, in this instance, left generations of devastation in its wake. The neglect will usually be coupled with a subtle and frightening expectation. The gifts of the parents must somehow be turned into a distinct and special advantage for the child. Eugene O'Neill's parents moved about in the way usual then among theatrical people. Mrs. O'Neill went along. The boy was put in boarding school at an early age. The successful, busy father and the weak, appealing mother—in Mrs. O'Neill's case, a drug addict. Eugene's brother, Jamie, became the most pathetic of alcoholics. He was a misbegotten creature, and died of drink at forty-five. Jamie had no gifts as an actor and yet, in as much as he worked at all, he worked on the stage, playing without distinction minor roles in productions in which his father was the star. Unlike Eugene, the other son did not have the talent or the sturdiness to withstand what seemed to have been unusual strains. Jamie was fond of his weak mother and pulled himself together briefly after James O'Neill died. But soon his mother died too, and Jamie, without any moral necessity left, quickly drank himself to death.

Eugene's youth and early theatrical career were spent under the shadow of his own intense alcoholism. Drink is a character in this tale, coming and going on the stage with fateful persistence. In his youth Eugene once attempted suicide and his drinking was always of the suicidal kind— oblivion sought in "Hell's Hole." The saving thing was his really extraordinary capacity for work. (Forty-five published plays are listed in the index made by Mr. and Mrs. Gelb.) O'Neill's character and his actions were very much of the 1920's; he was a typical artist of that time: radically removed, in one sense or another, from comfortable society, irresponsible, and yet wholly dedicated to art, persisting in work in spite of disastrous personal relations. There are fashions in lives as in works.

When Eugene O'Neill himself became a father, the tragedies of his own family were not only repeated but redoubled. He was strangely vindictive, monumentally neglectful. His first son, Eugene, Jr., was not a son at all in the early years of his life. O'Neill's first marriage had come about in the most careless, unromantic way, after the girl, Kathleen, became pregnant. (O'Neill's father wondered why she would want to marry a "drunken bum"—his son.) The divorce came quickly after the marriage. Kathleen later married again and O'Neill's son took his stepfather's name until, at the age of eleven, he learned his true identity, that he was Eugene O'Neill, Jr., the son of the famous dramatist. It is interesting to learn that Eugene, Jr., was doing rather badly until he discovered his real father. He reacted to this news by reform, trying to become worthy. He succeeded brilliantly for many years and then he, too, this most promising person, was compelled to destroy himself, first by drink, and then, literally, by suicide. In spite of his gifts and his hard work, the young O'Neill could not break the ice of his father's appalling self-concentration, his with-holding of himself, his really strange indifference. As it was, Eugene, Jr., came closer to his father than the two children by a second wife. Shane and Oona O'Neill seem to have been actually disliked by their father. Shane was weak and sensitive and deteriorated under the indifference. In his will, Eugene O'Neill cut off his children and their descendants from any share in his considerable property. He left it all to his third wife, Carlotta, and after her death to whatever heir she might want to choose.

O'Neill seems to have felt the claims of his parents and his brother more strongly than those of his children. He could feel sorrow for his mother's drug addiction, but seemed without pity for the addiction of his son. He could be sentimentally involved in the deterioration of Jamie; he lived in his own past, "a son and a brother." The Gelbs say, "O'Neill, father of three children, had no interest in the world his progeny would inhabit. He was occupied ex-clusively with the world that had shaped his forebears and himself. In his view the O'Neills ended with him." Per-haps his own successful creative life had made him harsh about weakness. O'Neill was shy, insecure and difficult; his steady effort to create significant dramatic works took everything out of him. He was restless and for the last decade of his life—for that at least—really ill. His third wife, Carlotta, seems, from these books, to have felt a possessive fidelity not without its own agonies for the self-consuming O'Neill. "Born in a hotel room and died in a hotel room," he is reported to have said of himself.

And the plays. They are nearly always singular and impressive and nearly always, in some detail or another, not quite realized. The editors of *O'Neill and his Plays* come down rather hard on the dissatisfied critics. "O'Neill's plays are particularly vulnerable to the newer critical methodology . . . There is an implication in Ferguson's discussion of Cummings' *him* that its inability to command an audience is somehow to its credit, and that, by contrast, O'Neill's ability to attract audiences to his plays is to his discredit."

One's doubts about O'Neill create a sense of guilt and unworthiness. A titan, an American! Awkward giants belittle us all. But there is no doubt that nearly every work of O'Neill's has blemishes—"lack of humor, sententiousness, sentimentality," Rosamund Gilder says in a friendly review of *The Iceman Cometh*. Lionel Trilling's very interesting and early essay on the "genius" of O'Neill puts his case very well when he speaks of "the power of genius itself, quite apart from its conclusions . . . In O'Neill, despite the many failures of his art and thought, this force is inescapable." George Jean Nathan thought the author of *Mourning Becomes Electra* "the most courageous, the most independently exploratory, the most ambitious and resourceful dramatist in the present day Anglo-American theatre." On the doubtful side consider: Eric Bentley's brilliant "Trying to Like O'Neill," Mary McCarthy on *The Iceman Cometh*, Edmund Wilson's description of the early plays as "rather second-rate naturalistic pieces that owe their eminence, not to their intrinsic greatness, but as Marx said of John Stuart Mill, 'to the flatness of the surrounding country.' " Wilson feels, however, that O'Neill is a sure artist when he creates characters from the lower classes, or the sea, those who speak in the vernacular.

Was it O'Neill or the European drama of Ibsen, Strindberg and Chekhov that freed American theater from falseness and gentility? Now, re-reading O'Neill's plays of forty years ago, the early ones, such as "*The Hairy Ape*," *All God's Chillun Got Wings*, one learns with surprise how persistent, how intrinsic perhaps, the strength and the weaknesses of O'Neill are in the American drama as a whole. Force, much true observation, a serious determination to turn the ugly material of American life into drama—these are the really moving particulars in O'Neill's struggle. And he is successful over and over as these plays, for the most part thrilling and true, step around those blocks of wood— the impossibly badly drawn characters, like the two women in "*The Hairy Ape*"—as if they were hurdles in a race. The very least one can say about *All God's Chillun* is that it is the best play about the drama of the Negro and the white race. (How tame *Deep Are the Roots* and other works written for the stage seem by comparison.) And *The Emperor Jones*, for all its "Who Dat?" dialogue, is a very successful masque, a pure bit of avant-garde theatre, not yet surpassed in this country. Yank, the pride-wounded stoker in "*The Hairy Ape*," is truly a symbolic creation; his descendants, in all their variations, have populated the American stage ever since and there is little chance they will die out soon.

The writing in the plays was thought by Hofmannsthal, an early admirer of O'Neill's, to fall short of the dialogue in Strindberg and Ibsen. Hofmannsthal wrote, ". . . the characters in O'Neill's plays seem to me a little too direct;

they utter the precise words demanded of them by the logic of the situation . . . they are not sufficiently drenched in the atmosphere of their own individual past." Perhaps that is it—for in the end the defects of really strong work are as hard to define as the strength. A certain humility is necessary about the lowly, badly hammered nails if the poor house, completed, moves you to tears. If the dialogue is so cumbersome how can the drama, projected through the dialogue, make its way into our senses?

The answer seems to lie in O'Neill's sincerity, his profound involvement in these plays. He went on and on and somehow he triumphed. The success of *Strange Interlude* is something like the success of Dreiser's *American Tragedy*. Sometimes literature is not made with words. It was a good instinct that told O'Neill to write long plays—the last thing one would ordinarily recommend for the unfelicitous, repetitious writer. *Strange Interlude* has some very bad writing. Nina speaks of "Giving her cool, clean body to men with hot hands and greedy eyes which they called love! Ugh!" (A shiver runs over her body.) The very title of the play comes in the dialogue at the end: "Strange interlude! Yes, our lives are merely strange dark interludes in the electrical display of God the Father!" And yet *Strange Interlude* is a convincing drama. The length is justified because the characters do change in a dramatic and life-like manner as they grow older, act after act. The young Sam Evans becomes, in a later act, the middle-aged, smug, wealthy Evans; Nina goes from hysteria to a period of domestic contentment and back to hysteria.

One thing is certain: in American drama O'Neill is preeminent. The extraordinary effect of *A Long Day's Journey* —the tale at last told of James O'Neill, the drug addict

mother, the drunkard Jamie, and the difficult Eugene himself—was a fitting requiem for this peculiar, heroic career.
T. S. Eliot thought it, "one of the most moving plays I
have ever seen."

1962

Locations

With Boston and its mysteriously enduring reputation, "the reverberation is longer than the thunderclap," as Emerson observed about the tenacious fame of certain artists. Boston —wrinkled, spindly-legged, depleted of nearly all her spiritual and cutaneous oils, provincial, self-esteeming—has gone on spending and spending her inflated bills of pure reputation, decade after decade. Now, one supposes it is all over at last. The old jokes embarrass, the anecdotes are so many thrice-squeezed lemons, and no new fruit hangs on the boughs. All the American regions are breaking up, ground down to a standard American corn meal. And why not Boston, which would have been the most difficult to maintain? There has never been anything quite like Boston as a creation of the American imagination, or perhaps one should say as a creation of the American scene. Some of the legend was once real, surely. Our utilitarian, fluid landscape has produced a handful of regional conceptions, popular images, brief and naked: the conservative Vermonter, the boastful Texan, the honeyed Southerner. "Graciousness is ours," brays a coarsened South; and the sheiks of Texas cruise around their desert.

The Boston image is more complex. The city is felt to

have, in the end, a pure and special nature, absurd no doubt
but somehow valuable. Empiricism will not carry one far;
faith and *being*, sheer being above all, are needed. To be it,
old Boston, real Boston, very Boston, and—one shrinks before the claim—proper Boston; there lies knowledge. An
author can hardly fail to turn a penny or two on this
magical subject. Everyone will consent to be informed on
it, to be slyly entertained by it. *Actual* Boston is governed
largely by people of Irish descent and more and more, recently, by men of Italian descent. Not long ago, the old
Yankee, Sentor Saltonstall, remarked wistfully that there
were still a good many Anglo-Saxons in Massachusetts, his
own family among them. Extinction is foreshadowed in
the defense.

Plainness and pretension restlessly feuding and combining; wealth and respectability and firmness of character
ending in the production of a number of diverting individual
tics or, at the best, instances of high culture—something of
that sort is the legendary Boston soul or so one supposes
without full confidence because the old citizens of Boston
vehemently hold to the notion that the city and their
character are ineffable, unknowable. When asked for an
opinion on the admirable novel, *Boston Adventure*, or even
the light social history, *The Proper Bostonian*, the answer
invariably comes, "Not Boston." The descriptive intelligence, the speculative mind, the fresh or even the merely
open eye are felt to discover nothing but errors here, be
they errors of praise or censure. Still, wrong-headedness
flourishes, the subject fascinates, and the Athenaeum's list
of written productions on this topic is nearly endless.

The best book on Boston is Henry James's novel, *The
Bostonians*. By the bald and bold use of the place name,
the unity of situation and person is dramatized. But poor

James, of course, was roundly and importantly informed by everyone, including his brother William, that this too was "not Boston." Stricken, he pushed aside a superb creation, and left the impregnable, unfathomable Boston to its mysteries. James's attitude toward the city's intellectual consequence and social charm is one of absolute impiety. A view of the Charles River reveals, ". . . an horizon indented at empty intervals with wooden spires, the masts of lonely boats, the chimneys of dirty 'works,' over a brackish expanse of anomalous character, which is too big for a river and too small for a bay." A certain house has "a peculiar look of being both new and faded—a kind of modern fatigue —like certain articles of commerce which are sold at a reduction as shopworn." However, there is little natural landscape in James's novel. The picture is, rather, of the psychological Boston of the 1870's, a confused scene, slightly mad with neurotic repressions, provincialism, and earnestness without intellectual seriousness.

James's view of Boston is not the usual one, although his irony and dissatisfaction are shared by Henry Adams, who says that "a simpler manner of life and thought could hardly exist, short of cave-dwelling," and by Santayana who spoke of Boston as a "moral and intellectual nursery, always busy applying first principles to trifles." The great majority of the writings on Boston are in another spirit altogether— they are frankly unctuous, for the town has always attracted men of quiet and timid and tasteful opinion, men interested in old families and things, in the charms of times recently past, collectors of anecdotes about those Boston worthies hardly anyone can still clearly identify, men who spoke and preached and whose fame deteriorated quickly. Rufus Choate, Dr. Channing, Edward Everett Hale, Phillips

Brooks, and Theodore Parker: names that remain in one's mind, without producing an image or a fact, as the marks are left on the wall after the picture has been removed. William Dean Howells held a more usual view than Henry James or Adams or Santayana. Indeed Howells's original enthusiasm for garden and edifice, person and setting, is more than a little *exalté*. The first sight of the Chapel at Mount Auburn Cemetery moved him more than the "Acropolis, Westminster Abbey, and Santa Croce in one." The massive gray stones of "the Public Library and the Athenaeum are hardly eclipsed by the Vatican and the Pitti." And so on.

The importance of Boston was intellectual and as its intellectual donations to the country have diminished, so it has declined from its lofty symbolic meaning, to become a more lowly image, a sort of farce of conservative exclusiveness and snobbish humor. Marquand's George Apley is a figure of the decline—fussy, sentimental, farcically mannered, archaic. He cannot be imagined as an Abolitionist, an author, a speaker; he is merely a "character." The old Boston had something of the spirit of Bloomsbury: it was clannish, worldly, and intellectually alive. About the historian, Prescott, Van Wyck Brooks could say, ". . . for at least ten years, Prescott had been hard at work, harder, perhaps, than any Boston merchant."

History, indeed, with its long, leisurely, gentlemanly labors, the books arriving by post, the cards to be kept and filed, the sections to be copied, the documents to be checked, is the ideal pursuit for the New England mind. All the Adamses spent a good deal of their lives on one kind of history or another. The eccentricity, studiousness, and study-window slow pace of life of the historical gentleman lay everywhere about the Boston scene. For money, society, fashion, extravagance, one went to New York. But now, the descendants of the old, intellectual aristocracy live in the respectable suburbs and lead the healthy, restless, outdoor life that atrophies the sedentary nerves of culture. The blue-stocking, the eccentric, the intransigent bring a blush of uncertainty and embarrassment to the healthy young couple's cheek.

Boston today can still provide a fairly stimulating atmosphere for the banker, the broker, for doctors and lawyers. "Open end" investments prosper, the fish come in at the dock, the wool market continues, and workers are employed in the shoe factories in the nearby towns. For the engineer, the physicist, the industrial designer, for all the highly trained specialists of the electronic age, Boston and its area are of seemingly unlimited promise. Sleek, well-designed factories and research centers pop up everywhere; the companies plead, in the Sunday papers, for more chemists, more engineers, and humbly relate the executive benefits of salary and pension and advancement they are prepared to offer.

But otherwise, for the artist, the architect, the composer, the writer, the philosopher, the historian, for those humane pursuits for which the town was once noted and even for the delights of entertainment, for dancing, acting, cooking, Boston is a bewildering place. There is, first of all, the question of Boston or New York. (The question is not new; indeed it was answered in the last decades of the last century in favor of New York as the cultural center of America.) It is, in our day, only a private and personal question: where or which of the two Eastern cities should one try to live and work in? It is a one-sided problem. For the New Yorker, San Francisco or Florida, perhaps—Boston, never. In Boston, New York tantalizes; one of the advantages of Boston is said, wistfully, to be its nearness to New York. It is a bad sign when a man, who has come to Boston or Cambridge, Massachusetts, from another place begins to show an undivided acceptance of his new town. Smugness is the great vice of the two places. Between puffy self-satisfaction and the fatiguing wonder if one wouldn't be happier, more productive, more appreciated in New York, a thoughtful man makes his choice.

Boston is not a small New York, as they say a child is not a small adult but is, rather, a specially organized small creature with its small-creature's temperature, balance, and distribution of fat. In Boston there is an utter absence of that wild electric beauty of New York, of the marvellous excited rush of people in taxicabs at twilight, of the great Avenues and Streets, the restaurants, theatres, bars, hotels, delicatessens, shops. In Boston the night comes down with an incredibly heavy, small-town finality. The cows come home; the chickens go to roost; the meadow is dark. Nearly every Bostonian is in his own house or in someone else's house, dining at the home board, enjoying domestic and social privacy. The "nice little dinner party"—for this the Bostonian would sell his soul. In the evenings, the old "accommodators" dart about the city, carrying their black uniforms and white aprons in a paper bag. They are on call to go anywhere, to cook and serve dinners. Many of these women are former cooks and maids, now living on Social Security retirement pensions, supplemented by the fees for these evening "accommodations" to the community. Their style and the bland respectability of their cuisine keep up the social tone of the town. They are like those old slaves who stuck to their places and, even in the greatest deprivation, graciously went on toting things to the Massa'.

There is a curious flimsiness and indifference in the commercial life of Boston. The restaurants are, charitably, to be called mediocre; the famous sea food is only palatable when raw. Otherwise it usually has to endure the deep-fry method that makes everything taste like the breaded pork chops of the Middle West, which in turn taste like the fried sole of Boston. Here, French restaurants quickly become tearoomy, as if some sort of rapid naturalization had taken place. There is not a single attractive eating place on the water front. An old downtown restaurant of considerable celebrity, Locke-Ober, has been expanded, let out, and "costumed" by one of the American restaurant decorators whose productions have a ready-make look, as if the designs had been chosen from a catalogue. But for the purest eccentricity, there is the "famous" restaurant, Durgin Park, which is run like a boardinghouse in a mining town. And so it goes. Downtown Boston at night is a dreary jungle of honky-tonks for sailors, dreary department store windows, Loew's movie houses, hillbilly bands, strippers, parking lots, undistinguished new buildings. Mid-town Boston—small, expensive shops, the inevitable Elizabeth Arden and Helena Rubinstein "salons," Brooks Brothers—is deserted at night, except for people going in and out of the Ritz Carlton Hotel, the only public place in Boston that could be called "smart." The merchandise in the Newbury Street shops is designed in a high fashion, elaborate, furred, and sequined, but it is never seen anywhere. Perhaps it is for out-of-town use, like a travelling man's mistress.

Just as there is no smart life, so there is no Soho, no Greenwich Village. Recently a man was murdered in a parking lot in the Chinatown area. His address was given as the South End, a lower-class section, and he was said to be a "free-spender," making enough money as a summer bartender on Cape Cod to lead a free-wheeling life the rest of the year. One paper referred to the unfortunate man as a "member of the Beacon Hill Bohemia set." This designation is of considerable interest because there is no "Bohemia" in Boston, neither upper nor lower; the detergent of bourgeois Boston cleans everything, effortlessly, completely. If there were a Bohemia, its members *would* live on Beacon Hill, the most beautiful part of Boston and, like the older parts of most cities, fundamentally classless, providing space for the rich in the noble mansions and for the people with little money in the run-down alleys. For both of these groups the walled gardens of Beacon Hill, the mews, the coach houses, the river views, the cobblestone streets are a necessity and the yellow brick structures of the Fenway are poison. *Espresso* bars have sprung up, or rather dug down in basements, but no summer of Bohemianism is ushered into town. This reluctance is due to the Boston legend and its endurance as a lost ideal, a romantic quest.

Something transcendental is always expected in Boston. There is, one imagines, behind the drapery on Mount Vernon Street a person of democratic curiosity and originality of expression, someone alas—and this is the tiresome Boston note—*wellborn*. It is likely to be, even in imagination, a *she*, since women now and not the men provide the links with the old traditions. Of her, then, one expects a certain unprofessionalism, but it is not expected that she will be superficial; she is profoundly conventional in manner of life but capable of radical insights. To live in Boston means to seek some connection with this famous local excellence, the regional type and special creation of the city.

An angry disappointment attends the romantic soul bent upon this quest. When the archaeological diggings do turn up an authentic specimen it will be someone old, nearly

gone, "whom you should have known when she was young"
—and could hear. The younger Bostonians seem in revolt
against the old excellence, with its indulgent, unfettered
development of the self. Revolt, however, is too active a
word for a passive failure to perpetuate the ideal high-
mindedness and intellectual effort. With the fashionable
young women of Boston, one might just as well be on
Long Island. In the nervous, shy, earnest women there is a
lingering hint of the peculiar local development. Terrible
faux pas are constantly being made by this reasonable, honorable person, followed by blushes and more false steps and
explanations and the final blinking, retreating blush.

Among the men, the equivalent of the blushing, blurting,
sensitive, and often "fine" woman, is a person who exists
everywhere perhaps but nowhere else with such elaboration
of type, such purity of example. This is the wellborn failure,
the amateur not by choice but from some fatal reticence of
temperament. They are often descendants of intellectual
Boston, odd-ball grandsons, charming and sensitive, puz-
zlingly complicated, living on a "small income." These unhappy men carry on their conscience the weight of unpublished novels, half-finished paintings, impossible historical
projects, old-fashioned poems, unproduced plays. Their inevitable "small income" is a sort of dynastic flaw, like
haemophilia. Much money seems often to impose obligations of energetic management; from great fortunes the
living cells receive the hints of the possibilities of genuine
power, enough even to make some enormously rich Americans endure the humiliations and fatigues of political office.
Only the most decadent and spoiled think of living in idleness on millions; but this notion does occur to the man
afflicted with ten thousand a year. He will commit himself
with a dreamy courage to whatever traces of talent he may

have and live to see himself punished by the New England conscience which demands accomplishments, duties performed, responsibilities noted, and energies sensibly used. The dying will accuses and the result is a queer kind of Boston incoherence. It is literally impossible much of the time to tell what some of the most attractive men in Boston are talking about. Half-uttered witticisms, grave and fascinating obfuscations, points incredibly qualified, hesitations infinitely refined—one staggers about, charmed and confused by the twilight.

But this person, with his longings, connects with the old possibilities and, in spite of his practical failure, keeps alive the memory of the best days. He may have a brother who has retained the mercantile robustness of nature and easy capacity for action and yet has lost all belief in anything except money and class, who may practice private charities, but entertains profoundly trivial national and world views. A Roosevelt, Harriman, or Stevenson are impossible to imagine as members of the Boston aristocracy; here the vein of self-satisfaction and public indifference cuts too deeply.

Harvard (across the river in Cambridge) and Boston are two ends of one mustache. Harvard is now so large and international it has altogether avoided the whimsical stagnation of Boston. But the two places need each other, as we knowingly say of a mismatched couple. Without the faculty, the visitors, the events that Harvard brings to the life here, Boston would be intolerable to anyone except genealogists, antique dealers, and those who find repletion in a closed local society.

Unfortunately, Harvard, like Boston, has "tradition," and in America this always carries with it the risk of a special staleness of attitude, and of pride, incredibly and comically swollen like the traits of hypocrisy, selfishness, or lust in the old dramas. At Harvard some of the vices of "society" exist, of Boston society that is—arrogance and the blinding dazzle of being, *being at Harvard*. The moral and social tempta- tions of Harvard's unique position in American academic life are great and the pathos is seen in those young faculty mem- bers who are presently at Harvard but whose appointments are not permanent and so they may be thrown down, banished from the beatific condition. The young teachers in this position live in a dazed state of love and hatred, pride and fear; their faces have a look of desperate yearning, for they would rather serve in heaven than reign in hell. For those who are not banished, for the American at least, since the many distinguished foreigners at Harvard need not en- dure these piercing and fascinating complications, something of Boston seems to seep into their characters. They may come from anywhere in America and yet to be at Harvard unites them with the transcendental, legendary Boston, with New England in flower. They begin to revere the old worthies, the houses, the paths trod by so many before, and they feel a throb of romantic sympathy for the directly- gazing portraits on the walls, for the old graves and old names in the Mount Auburn Cemetery. All of this has charm and may even have a degree of social and intellectual value—and then again it may not. Devious parochialisms, irrelevant snobberies, a bemused exaggeration of one's own produc- tions, pimple the soul of a man upholding tradition in a forest of relaxation, such as most of America is thought to be. Henry James's observation in his book on Hawthorne bears on this:

> . . . it is only in a country where newness and change and brevity of tenure are the common substance of life, that the fact of one's ancestors having lived for a hundred and

seventy years in a single spot would become an element of
one's morality. It is only an imaginative American that would
feel urged to keep reverting to this circumstance, to keep
analysing and cunningly considering it.

If the old things of Boston are too heavy and plushy,
the new either hasn't been born or is appallingly shabby
and poor. As early as Thanksgiving, Christmas decorations
unequaled for cheap ugliness go up in the Public Garden
and on the Boston Common. Year after year, the city fathers
bring out crêches and camels and Mother and Child so
badly made and of such tasteless colors they verge on
blasphemy, or would seem to do so if it were not for the
further degradation of secular little men blowing horns and
the canes of peppermint hanging on the lamps. The shock
of the first sight is the most interesting; later the critical
senses are stilled as year after year the same bits are brought
forth and gradually one realizes that the whole thing is a
sort of permanent exhibition.

Recently the dying downtown shopping section of Boston
was to be graced with flowers, an idea perhaps in imitation
of the charming potted geraniums and tulips along Fifth
Avenue in New York. Commercial Boston produced a really
amazing display: old, gray square bins, in which were stuck
a few bits of yellowing, dying evergreen. It had the look
of exhausted greenery thrown out in the garbage and soon
the dustbins were full of other bits of junk and discard—
people had not realized or recognized the decorative hope
and saw only the rubbishy result.

The municipal, civic backwardness of Boston does not
seem to bother its more fortunate residents. For them and
for the observer, Boston's beauty is serene and private, an
enclosed, intense personal life, rich with domestic variation,

interesting stuffs and things, showing the hearthside vitality of a Dutch genre painting. Of an evening the spirits quicken, not to public entertainment, but instead to the sights behind the draperies, the glimpses of drawing rooms on Louisburg Square, paneled walls and French chandeliers on Commonwealth Avenue, bookshelves and flower-filled bays on Beacon Street. Boston is a winter city. Every apartment has a fireplace. In the town houses, old persons climb steps without complaint, four or five floors of them, cope with the maintenance of roof and gutter and survive the impractical kitchen and resign themselves to the useless parlors. This is life; the house, the dinner party, the charming gardens, one's high ceilings, fine windows, lacy grillings, magnolia trees, inside shutters, glassed-in studios on the top of what were once stables, outlook on the "river side." Setting is serious. When it is not serious, when a splendid old private house passes into less dedicated hands, an almost exuberant swiftness of deterioration can be noticed. A rooming house, although privately owned, is no longer in the purest sense a private house and soon it partakes of some of the feckless, ugly, municipal neglect. The contrasts are startling. One of two houses of almost identical exterior design will have shining windows, a bright brass door knocker, and its twin will show a *"Rooms"* sign peering out of dingy glass, curtained by those lengths of flowered plastic used in the shower bath. Garbage lies about in the alleys behind the rooming houses, discarded furniture blocks old garden gateways. The vulnerability of Boston's way of life, the meanness of most things that fall outside the needs of the upper classes, are shown with a bleak and terrible fullness in the rooming houses on Beacon Street. And even some of the best houses show a spirit of mere "maintenance," which, while useful for the individual with money, leads to civic dullness, architectural torpor, and stagnation. In the Back Bay area, a voluntary, casual association of property owners exists for the purpose of trying to keep the alleys clean, the streets lighted beyond their present medieval darkness, and to pursue other worthy items of neighborhood value. And yet this same group will "protest" against the attractive Café Florian on Newbury Street (smell of coffee too strong!) and against the brilliantly exciting Boston Arts Festival held in the beautiful Public Garden for two weeks in June. The idea that Boston might be a vivacious, convenient place to live in is not uppermost in these residents' thoughts. Trying to buy groceries in the best section of the Back Bay region is an interesting study in commercial apathy.

A great many of the young Bostonians leave town, often taking off with a sullen demand for a freer, more energetic air. And yet many of them return later, if not to the city itself, to the beautiful sea towns and old villages around it. For the city itself, who will live in it after the present human landmarks are gone? No doubt, some of the young people there at the moment will persevere, and as a reward for their fidelity and endurance will themselves later become monuments, old types interesting to students of what our colleges call American Civilization. Boston is defective, out-of-date, vain, and lazy, but if you're not in a hurry it has a deep, secret appeal. Or, more accurately, those who like it may make of its appeal a secret. The weight of the Boston legend, the tedium of its largely fraudulent posture of traditionalism, the disillusionment of the Boston present as a cultural force make quick minds hesitate to embrace a region too deeply compromised. They are on their guard against falling for it, but meanwhile they can enjoy its very defects, its backwardness, its slowness, its position as one of the large, possible cities on the Eastern seacoast, its private, residential charm. They speak of going to New York and yet another season finds them holding back, positively enjoying the Boston life. . . .

. . . Outside it is winter, dark. The curtains are drawn, the wood is on the fire, the table has been checked, and in the stillness one waits for the guests who come stamping in out of the snow. There are lectures in Cambridge, excellent concerts in Symphony Hall, bad plays being tried out for the hungry sheep of Boston before going to the hungry sheep of New York. Arnold Toynbee or T. S. Eliot or Robert Frost or Robert Oppenheimer or Barbara Ward is in town again. The cars are double-parked so thickly along the narrow streets that a moving vehicle can scarcely maneuver; the pedestrians stumble over the cobbles; in the back alleys a cat cries and the rats, enormously fat, run in front of the car lights creeping into the parking spots. Inside it is cosy, Victorian, and gossipy. Someone else has *not* been kept on at Harvard. The old Irish "accommodator" puffs up stairs she had never seen before a few hours previously and announces that dinner is ready. A Swedish journalist is just getting off the train at the Back Bay Station. He has been exhausted by cocktails, reality, life, taxis, telephones, bad connections in New York and Chicago, pulverized by a "good time." Sighing, he alights, seeking old Boston, a culture that hasn't been alive for a long time . . . and rest.

1959

13 / A Florentine Conference

The guests were leaving and the house was cold. It was near midnight. Outside Florence was quiet, pale yellow with damp, shining streets, an immense barracks of tall, dusty-shuttered houses, calm and solemn with privacy. An old horse stumbled over the cobbles, jerking behind him a frozen driver and an empty black and green carriage of remarkable endurance.

"Make no mistake they can take over in twenty-four hours, don't fool yourself," Miss Major said, pulling on her wool-lined gloves and addressing the room with glowing, pink-cheeked anxiety and oracular brevity.

"They?" Marchese Ferrero said. This young man had not been following Miss Major, but had instead been discussing the departure for America of another young Italian whose name was of such antique beginnings and miraculous survival in the indescribable splendor of Florentine snobbery that merely to utter it was a cultural act, like a recitation from Tasso. "What can Nicky do there, I wonder? I wonder very much. . . . He likes fishing and hunting and is charming, charming, but still you know . . . America. . . ." The Marchese spoke English with an excellent Oxford accent and from time to time his nose lifted timidly into the air, as if it were flying south for a holiday.

In Italian someone said, "Igor Cassini did quite well there. . . . And the old Italian in California, with the bank, you know. . . . Perhaps they can. . . . Nicky is adored by everyone. . . ."

"Cassini, yes, many connections, but still. . . . And the old man in California is dead, isn't he, and no one seems to know *him* anyway. . . ."

"Fiorello La Guardia" another voice added and the Italians laughed. "Fiorello!"

"In twenty-four hours and any time they want to . . . from within, I mean. . . ." Miss Major repeated thoughtfully.

"*They?* Oh yes, the Communists. . . . Of course. . . . In twenty-four hours, you know so? Not even a few days, eh?" The Marchese suddenly turned quite red with humiliation. His fine eyes blinked sadly and he looked shyly, cautiously, about the room, as if to say, "Dear friends, you are mad with me, perhaps? No. . . . No, really? Many thanks, please!"

An American who made propaganda films for the American government, a sharp-chinned man with a faded, clever face and a faded brown mustache, glared at the empty white and gold coffee cups with a fury somewhat bored by its own violence. This photographer felt deeply the stab of professional insult common to people who have lived in a foreign country for a few years and *still* find their opinions not asked for at home. His little face, all of it, all at once, frowned with injury. "Our policy is hopeless! De Gasperi's hands are tied because he needs the financial support of the landowners and when you depend upon that support you aren't likely to set about land reform with any great speed—"

"Ah, yes, slow and modest . . . but a very good man, a good honest fellow, I understand, De Gasperi?" the Marchese said vaguely.

"*We* ought to back De Gasperi with some of the money we're pouring into the wrong places, back him and tell him to go ahead with the reforms." The photographer's eyes now menaced the heavy silver ornaments on the desk before him. He sighed and shrugged, bone weary with his government, that fractious wife driving him to divorce.

"But have we the right . . . the right?" an old American expatriate wondered, a large, wrinkled woman in a worn, spotted fur coat from some animal strange to modern eyes. "It's easy to say come in and divide up a bit of land here and there, yes . . . but is it? Can we, just like that? It's not our country and the interference—"

"My dear goose," the photographer said icily in that awful tone of passionate domestic quarrel, raw with the ultimate provocation, "it isn't as if millions of dollars to the Fiat Company weren't interference!"

The fire was almost out. A hoarse-voiced Italian with magnificent wavy hair, tough, durable and fierce as cactus, said to the photographer's sister who had just arrived for her first visit to Italy, "Are there any interesting writers in Italy? Horrors, what a question! Bah! Does a dead man write? . . . We're just a few old rattling bones. . . . The future, ugh! It's America's turn now. . . . It's all yours. . . . I give it to you! Bah!"

The girl blushed with genuine modesty, a virgin shrinking from the bad taste of an overwhelming offer. "No, really, I don't think you should say that! . . . It's lovely here. . . . Honestly!"

Marchese Ferrero attempted lightness. "We may revive someday. . . . Look at China!"

"Twenty-four hours. They've incredible discipline," Miss Major went on. "It's something to watch, right here even. The Mayor of Florence was trained in Moscow, you see. . . . You see?"

"Oh, Madge!" the old expatriate lady said. "Don't laugh at me. . . . I'm as sentimental as a dove, yes, but Florence! The Duomo, the Uffizi, Donatello and the rest, Santa Croce . . . The Medici, things like that! In Moscow you say, dear . . . Extraordinary. The Mayor of Florence!" She coughed and pondered bleakly, stiff with a half-century of Italian winters. This gentle Florentine relic had only a modest stipend, just enough to see her through years and years in the arctic chambers of the Biblioteca Nazionale and the library of the British Institute. There she was "working" on her favorites among the great Italian women—Bianca Capello, Vittoria Colonna and Isabella D'Este—and with terrible patience digging away at these figures' awesome heroism, down, down to the pure ore, which this old scholar, rheum-eyed with labor, saw in the dim shape of her own fatigued fortitude and stubborn competence. These diggings and strikes brought the battered American lady all the consolations of religion and philosophy.

"Mmm . . ." the photographer said indifferently, shuddering at the obsolescence of his compatriot who had now turned her book-weary face to him, as if for protection.

An old servant, an immense woolen creature, a sort of quartermaster corps on two legs, padded and stuffed with underwear and mysterious layers from head to toe, bowed them out. When they had gone, she sleepily peered through the shutters and looked down at the wind disturbing the muddy flow of the Arno. In the moonlight, the derricks and tanks, rebuilding the Ponte alla Carraia which had been blown up by the Germans in 1944, shone like silver. Muttering her evening complaints and prayers the servant went off to bed, pulled a mountain of covers, old sheets and stuffings up to her neck and, turning now on her side, fell into a blessed, illiterate sleep.

1951

Vassal, slave, inferior, other, thing, victim, dependent, parasite, prisoner—oh, bitter, raped, child-swollen flesh doomed to immanence! Sisyphean goddess of the dust pile! Demeter, Xantippe, Ninon de Lenclos, Marie Bashkirtsev, and "a friend of mine . . ." From cave to café, boudoir to microscope, from the knitting needles to the short story: they are all here in a potency of pages, a foreshortened and exaggerated, a mysterious and too clear relief, an eloquent lament and governessy scolding, a poem and a doctoral thesis. I suppose there is bound to be a little laughter in the wings at the mere thought of this madly sensible and brilliantly obscure tome on women by Simone de Beauvoir, *The Second Sex.*

Still the more one sinks into this very long book, turning page after page, the more clearly it seems to lack a subject with reasonable limitations and concreteness, a subject on which offered illustrations may wear some air of finality and conviction. The theme of the work is that women are not simply "women," but are, like men, in the fullest sense human beings. Yet one cannot easily write the history of people! This point may appear trivial; nevertheless, to take

A review of *The Second Sex* by Simone de Beauvoir.

on this glorious and fantastic book is not like reading at all—
from the first to the last sentence one has the sensation of
playing some breathlessly exciting and finally exhausting
game. You gasp and strain and remember; you point out
and deny and agree, trying always to find some way of
taking hold, of confining, defining, and understanding. What
is so unbearably whirling is that the author too goes through
this effort to include nearly every woman and attitude
that has ever existed. There is no difference of opinion, unless it be based upon a fact of which she may be ignorant,
she has not thought of also. She makes her own points and
all one's objections too, often in the same sentence. The
effort required for this work must have been killing. No
discredit to the donkey-load undertaking is meant when one
imagines Simone de Beauvoir at the end may have felt
like George Eliot when she said she began *Romola* as a
young woman and finished it an old one. (This touching
remark did not refer to the time spent in composition, but
to the wrinkling weight of the task.)

I quote a sentence about the *promises* the Soviet Union
made to women: ". . . pregnancy leaves were to be paid
for by the State, which would assume charge of the children,
signifying not that they would be *taken away* from their
parents, but that they would not be *abandoned* to them."
There is majesty here and the consolations of philosophy,
perhaps also, in this instance, a bit of willful obfuscation;
but that kind of strangeness occurs endlessly, showing, for
purposes of argument at least, an oversensitivity to difficulties. A devastating dialogue goes on at this author's
desk. After she has written, "the State, which would assume
charge of the children," there is a comma pause. In that
briefest of grammatical rests, voices assault her intelligence
saying, "But suppose people don't want their children

taken away by the State?" If all these disputing voices are admitted, one on top of the other, you are soon lost in incoherence and fantasy. Another instance: "It is understandable, in this perspective, that women take exception to masculine logic. Not only is it inapplicable to her experience, but in his hands, as she knows, masculine reasoning becomes an underhanded form of force." A few pages on: "One can bank on her credulity. Woman takes an attitude of respect and faith toward the masculine universe . . ."

I take up the bewildering inclusiveness of this book, because there is hardly a thing I would want to say contrary to her thesis that Simone de Beauvoir has not said herself, including the fact, mentioned in the preface, that problems peculiar to women are not particularly pressing at the moment and that, by and large, "we have won." These acknowledgments would seem of tremendous importance, but they are a mere batting of the eye in this eternity of "oppression."

In spite of all positions being taken simultaneously, there is an unmistakable *drift* to the book. Like woman's life, *The Second Sex* is extremely repetitious and some things are repeated more often than others, although nearly every idea is repeated more than once. One is justified, then, in assuming what is repeated most often is most profoundly felt. The diction alone is startling and stabs the heart with its vigor in finding phrases of abjection and debasement. It is as though one had lived forever in that intense, shady, wretched world of *Wozzeck*, where the humor draws tears, the gaiety is fearful and children skip rope neither knowing nor caring their mother has been murdered. "Conjugal slavery, annihilation, servant, devaluation, tyranny, passive, forbidden, doomed, abused, trapped, prey, domineer, helpless, imprisoned," and so on. This immediately suggests a masochistic view of life, reinforced by the fact that for the male quite an opposite vocabulary has dug into this mind like a tick: "free, busy, active, proud, arrogant, master, existent, liberty, adventure, daring, strength, courage . . ."

Things being as they are, it is only fair to say that Simone de Beauvoir, in spite of her absorbing turn of phrase, miraculously does *not* give to me, at least, the impression of being a masochist, a Lesbian, a termagant, or a man-hater, and that this book is not "the self-pitying cry of one who resents being born a woman," as one American housewife-reviewer said. There is a nervous, fluent, rare aliveness on every page and the writer's more "earnest" qualities, her discipline, learning and doggedness, amount not only to themselves, that is, qualities which certainly help one to write long books, but to a kind of "charm" that ought to impress the most contented woman. This book is an accomplishment; on the other hand, if one is expecting something truly splendid and unique like *The Origins of Totalitarianism* by Hannah Arendt, to mention another woman, he will be disappointed.

The Second Sex begins with biological material showing that in nature there are not always two sexes and reproduction may take place asexually. I have noticed in the past that many books strongly presenting feminine claims begin in this manner, as if under a compulsion to veil the whole idea of sexual differentiation with a buzzing, watery mist of insect habits and unicellular forms of life. This is dramaturgy, meant to put one, after a heavy meal, in a receptive frame of mind. It is the dissonant, ambiguous music as the curtain rises on the all too familiar scene of the man at the hunt and the woman at the steaming pot; the scene looks clear enough, but the music suggests things may not be as they appear. That woman may not have to carry those screaming brats in her womb, after all, but will, if you don't watch out, simply "divide"! And the man: it is possible in the atomic age that a pin prick may fertilize the egg and then where will he be? This material is followed by curiosities from anthropology: some primitive societies thought the woman did it all alone and the man was no more important than a dish of herbs or a draft of beet juice.

These biological and anthropological matters are of enormous fascination, but often, and a bit in this present work too, a false and dramatic use is made of them: they carry a weight of mystification and intensity quite unjustified when the subject is the modern woman. They would seem to want to throw doubt upon what is not yet doubtful: the bisexual nature of human reproduction. We are relieved when the dividing amoebas and budding sponges swim out of view.

The claim of *The Second Sex* is that what we call the feminine character is an illusion and so is feminine "psychology," both in its loose meaning and in the psychoanalytical view. None of these female traits is "given"—the qualities and incapacities women have shown rather consistently in human history are simply the result of their "situation." This situation is largely the work of men, the male sex which has sought its own convenience with undeviating purpose throughout history. The female situation does not derive, at least not sufficiently to explain it, from women's natural physical and psychological difference, but has much of its origin in economics. When man developed the idea of private property, woman's destiny was "sealed." At this time women were cut off from the more adventurous activities of war, forays, explorations, to stay at home to *protect* and *maintain* what men had achieved by their far-reaching pursuits. The woman was reduced to a state of *immanence:* stagnation, the doing of repetitive tasks, concerned with the given, with maintaining, keeping, mere functioning. Man, however, is a free being, an *existent* who makes choices, decisions, has projects which are not confined to securing the present but point to the unknown future; he dares, fails, wanders, grabs, insists. By means of his activities he *transcends* his mere animal nature. What a man gives, the woman accepts; she decides nothing, changes nothing; she polishes, mends, cleans what he has invented and shaped. The man risks life, the woman merely produces it as an unavoidable function. "That is why superiority has been accorded in humanity not to the sex that brings forth but that which kills." The man imagines, discovers religions; the women worship. He has changed the earth; she arises each morning to an expectation of stove, nursing, scrubbing which has remained nearly as fixed as the course of our planets. Women continue in immanence not out of desire, but from "complicity." Having been robbed of economic independence, experience, substance, she clings unhappily because she has not been "allowed" to prepare for a different life.

Naturally, it is clear many women do not fit this theory and those who may be said to do so would not describe it in the words of Simone de Beauvoir. These persons' claims are admitted quite fully throughout the book, but always with the suggestion that the women who seem to be "existents" really aren't and those who insist they find fulfillment in the inferior role are guilty of "bad faith."

That is as it may be, but what, one asks at the beginning, about the man who, almost without exception in this work, is a creature of the greatest imagination, love of liberty, devotion to projects; ambitious, potent and disciplined, he scorns a life of mere "love," refuses to imprison himself in another's being, but looks toward the world, seeks to transcend himself, change the course of history. This is an exaggeration of course. For every Ophelia one remembers not only Cleopatra but poor Swann, unable, for all his taste and enthusiasm, to write his book on Vermeer, drowning his talent in the pursuit of pure pleasure which can only be given by the "other," Odette; for every excited Medea who gave up herself, her place, to follow the fickle man you remember not only Joan of Arc but that being of perfect, blowsy immanence, the Duke of Windsor, who abandoned the glories of a complex project for the sweet, repetitive, futureless domesticity of ocean liners and resorts. And Sartre has written a whole book on Baudelaire, a fascinating and immensely belligerent one, that claims Beaudelaire resented responsibility for his own destiny, refused his possibilities of transcendence, would not make decisions, define himself, but flowed along on a tepid river of dependence, futility, refusal—like women, fond of scents and costumes, nostalgic, procrastinating, wishful.

It would seem then that men, even some "heroic" ones, often allow themselves to be what women are forced to be. But, of course, with the greatest will in the world a man cannot allow himself to be that most extremely doomed and chained being—the mother who must bear and raise children and whose figure naturally hangs over such a work as *The Second Sex* like Spanish moss. Simone de Beauvoir's opinion of the division of labor established in the Garden of Eden, if not as some believe earlier, is very striking:

> . . . giving birth and suckling are not *activities*, they are natural functions; no projects are involved; and that is why woman found in them no reason for a lofty affirmation of her existence—she submitted passively to her biologic fate. The

domestic cares of maternity imprisoned her in repetition and immanence; they were repeated from day to day in an identical form, which was perpetuated almost without change from century to century; they produced nothing new.

But what difference does it make that childbearing is not an activity, nor perhaps an instinct; it is a necessity.

The Second Sex is so briskly Utopian it fills one with a kind of shame and sadness, like coming upon old manifestoes and committee programs in the attic. It is bursting with an almost melancholy desire for women to take their possibilities *seriously*, to reject the given, the easy, the traditional. I do not, as most reviewers seem to, think the picture offered here of a woman's life is entirely false—a lifetime of chores is bad luck. But housework, child rearing, cleaning, keeping, nourishing, looking after—these must be done by someone, or worse by millions of someones day in and day out. In the home at least it would seem "custom" has not been so much capricious as observant in finding that women are fairly well adapted to this necessary routine. And they must keep at it whether they like it or not.

George Orwell says somewhere that reformers hate to admit nobody will do the tedious, dirty work of the world except under "some form of coercion." Mopping, ironing, peeling, feeding—it is not absurd to call this unvarying routine *slavery*, Simone de Beauvoir's word. But its necessity does not vanish by listing the tropical proliferation of open and concealed forms of coercion that may be necessary to make women do it. Bachelors are notoriously finicky, we have all observed. The dust pile is revoltingly real.

Most men, also, are doomed to work of brutalizing monotony. Hardly any intellectuals are willing to undertake a bit of this dreadful work their fellow beings must do, no matter what salary, what working conditions, what degree of "socialist dignity" might be attached to it. If artists could save a man from a lifetime of digging coal by digging it themselves one hour a week, most would refuse. Some would commit suicide. "It's not the time, it's the anticipation! It ruins the whole week! I can't even read, much less write!"

Childbearing and housekeeping may be repetitive and even intellectually stunting. Yet nothing so fills one with despair as those products of misplaced transcendent hope, those millions of stupid books, lunatic pamphlets, absurd editorials, dead canvases and popular songs which have clogged up the sewers and ashcans of the modern world, representing more wretched labor, dreaming, madness, vanity and waste of effort than one can bear to think of. There is an annihilating nothingness in these undertakings by comparison with which the production of one stupid, lazy, lying child is an event of some importance. Activity, transcendence, project—this is an optimistic, exhilarating vocabulary. Yet Sartre had to disown the horde of "existents" who fell to like farm hands at the table, but were not themselves able to produce so much as a carrot.

Are women "the equal" of men? This is an embarrassing subject.

Women are certainly physically inferior to men and if this were not the case the whole history of the world would be different. No comradely socialist legislation on woman's behalf could accomplish a millionth of what a bit more muscle tissue, gratuitously offered by nature, might do for this "second" being.

On the average she is shorter than the male and lighter, her skeleton is more delicate . . . muscular strength is much less in women . . . she has less respiratory capacity, the lungs and trachea being smaller . . . The specific gravity of the blood is lower . . . and there is less hemoglobin; women are therefore less robust and more disposed to anemia than are males. Their pulse is more rapid, the vascular system less stable . . . Instability is strikingly characteristic of woman's organization in general . . . In comparison with her the male seems infinitely favored.

There is a kind of poetry in this description which might move a flighty person to tears. But it goes on:

These biological considerations are extremely important . . . But I deny that they establish for her a fixed and inevitable destiny. They are insufficient for setting up a hierarchy of the sexes . . . they do not condemn her to remain in a subordinate role forever.

Why doesn't this "condemn her to remain in a subordinate role forever"? In my view this poor endowment would seem to be all the answer one needs to why women don't sail the seven seas, build bridges, conquer foreign lands, lay international cables and trudge up Mount Everest. But forgetting these daring activities, a woman's physical inferiority to a man is a limiting reality every moment of her life. Because of it women are "doomed" to situations that promise reasonable safety against the more hazardous possibilities of nature which they are too weak and easily fatigued to endure and against the stronger man. Any woman who has ever had her wrist twisted by a man recognizes a fact of nature as humbling as a cyclone to a frail tree branch. How can *anything* be more important than this? The prodigious ramifications could occupy one for an eternity. For instance:

> At eighteen T. E. Lawrence took a long bicycle tour through France by himself; no young girl would be allowed to engage in any escapade, still less to adventure on foot in a half-desert and dangerous country, as Lawrence did a year later.

Simone de Beauvoir's use of "allow" is inaccurate; she stresses "permission" where so often it is really "capacity" that is involved. For a woman a solitary bicycle tour of France would be dangerous, but not impossible; Lawrence's adventure in Arabia would be suicidal and so a woman is nearly unimaginable as the author of *The Seven Pillars of Wisdom*. First of all the Arabs would rape this unfortunate female soldier or, if they had some religious or practical reason for resisting temptation, they would certainly have to leave her behind on the march, like yesterday's garbage, as the inevitable fatigue arrived. To say that physical weakness doesn't, in a tremendous number of activities, "condemn her to a subordinate role" is a mere assertion, not very convincing to the unmuscled, light breathing, nervously unstable, blushing feminine reality.

Arabian warfare is indeed an extreme situation. But what about solitary walks through the town after midnight? It is true that a woman's freedom to enjoy this simple pleasure would be greatly increased if men had no aggressive sexual feelings toward her. Like a stray dog, also weaker than men, she might roam the world at will, arousing no more notice than a few pats on the head or an irritable kick now and then. Whether such a change is possible in the interest of the weaker sex is very doubtful.

There is the notion in *The Second Sex*, and in other radical books on the subject, that if it were not for the tyranny of custom, women's sexual life would be characterized by the same aggressiveness, greed and command as that of the male.

This is by no means certain: so much seems to lead right back where we've always been. Society must, it seems, inhibit to some extent the sexuality of all human beings. It has succeeded in restraining men much less than women. Brothels, which have existed from the earliest times, are to say the least a rarity for the use of women. And yet women will patronize opium dens and are frequently alcoholic, activities wildly destructive to their home life, beauty, manners and status and far more painful and time-consuming than having children. Apparently a lot of women are dying for dope and cocktails; nearly all are somewhat thrifty, cautious and a little lazy about hunting sex. Is it necessarily an error that many people think licentious women are incapable of experiencing the slightest degree of sexual pleasure and are driven to their behavior by an encyclopedic curiosity to know if such a thing exists? A wreck of a man, tracking down girls in his Chevrolet, at least can do *that!* Prostitutes are famously cold; pimps, who must also suffer professional boredom, are not automatically felt to be impotent. Homosexual women, who have rebelled against their "conditioning" in the most crucial way, do not appear to "cruise" with that truly astonishing, ageless zest of male homosexuals. A pair seems to find each other sufficient. Drunken women who pick up a strange man look less interested in a sexual partner than in a companion for a drink the next morning. There is a staggering amount of evidence that points to the idea that women set a price of one kind or another on sexual intercourse; they are so often not in the mood.

This is not to say women aren't interested in sex *at all.* They clearly want a lot of it, but in the end the men of the world seem to want still more. It is only the quantity, the capacity in that sense, in which the sexes appear to differ. Women, in the language of sociology books, "fight very

hard" to get the amount of sexual satisfaction they want—
and even harder to keep men from forcing a superabundance
their way. It is difficult to see how anyone can be sure that
it is only man's voracious appetite for conquest which has
created, as its contrary, this reluctant, passive being who has
to be wooed, raped, bribed, begged, threatened, married,
supported. Perhaps she really has to be. After she has been
conquered she has to "pay" the man to restrain his appetite,
which he is so likely to reveal at cocktail parties, and in his
pitifully longing glance at the secretary—she pays with
ironed shirts, free meals, the pleasant living room, a son.

And what about the arts—those womanish activities which
are, in our day, mostly "done at home." For those who
desire this form of transcendence, the other liberating activities of mankind, the office, the factory, the world of commerce, public affairs, are horrible pits where the extraordinary man is basely and casually slain.

Women have excelled in the performance arts: acting,
dancing and singing—for some reason Simone de Beauvoir
treats these accomplishments as if they were usually an extension of prostitution. Women have contributed very little
to the art of painting and they are clearly weak in the gift
for musical composition. (Still whole nations seem without
this latter gift, which may be inherited. Perhaps even nations
inherit it, the male members at least. Like baldness, women
may transmit the gift of musical composition but they seldom ever suffer from it.)

Literature is the art in which women have had the greatest
success. But a woman needs only to think of this activity
to feel her bones rattling with violent distress. Who is to say
that *Remembrance of Things Past* is "better" than the marvelous *Emma*? *War and Peace* better than *Middlemarch*?

Moby Dick superior to *La Princesse de Clèves?* But every-body says so! It is only the whimsical, cantankerous, the eccentric critic, or those who refuse the occasion for such distinctions, who would say that any literary work by a woman, marvelous as these may be, is on a level with the very greatest accomplishments of men. Of course the *best* literature by women is superior to *most* of the work done by men and anyone who values literature at all will approach all excellence with equal enthusiasm.

The Second Sex is not whimsical about women's writing, but here again perhaps too much is made of the position in which women have been "trapped" and not enough of how "natural" and inevitable their literary limitations are. Never-theless, the remarks on artistic women are among the most brilliant in this book. Narcissism and feelings of inferiority are, according to Simone de Beauvoir, the demons of literary women. Women want to please, "but the writer of origi-nality, unless dead, is always shocking, scandalous; novelty disturbs and repels." Flattered to be in the world of art at all, the woman is "on her best behavior; she is afraid to disarrange, to investigate, to explode . . ." Women are timid and fall back on "ancient houses, sheepfolds, kitchen gardens, picturesque old folks, roguish children . . ." and even the best are conservative. "There are women who are mad and there are women of sound method; none has that madness in her method that we call genius."

If women's writing seems somewhat limited, I don't think it is only due to these psychological failings. Women have much less experience of life than a man, as everyone knows. But in the end are they suited to the kind of experiences men have? *Ulysses* is not just a work of genius, it is Dublin pubs, gross depravity, obscenity, brawls. Stendhal as a soldier in Napoleon's army, Tolstoy on his Cossack campaigns, Dostoevsky before the firing squad, Proust's obviously first-hand knowledge of vice, Conrad and Melville as sailors, Michelangelo's tortures on the scaffolding in the Sistine chapel, Ben Jonson's drinking bouts, dueling, his ear burnt by the authorities because of a political indiscretion in a play—these horrors and the capacity to endure them are *experience*. Experience is something more than going to law school or having the nerve to say honestly what you think in a drawing room filled with men; it is the privilege as well to endure brutality, physical torture, unimaginable sordidness, and even the privilege *to want*, like Boswell, to grab a miserable tart under Westminster Bridge. Syphilis and epilepsy—even these seem to be tragic afflictions a male writer can endure more easily than a woman. I should imagine a woman would be more depleted by epilepsy than Dostoevsky seems to have been, more ravaged by syphilis than Flaubert, more weakened by deprivation than Villon. Women live longer, safer lives than men and a man may, if he wishes, choose that life; it is hard to believe a woman could choose, like Rimbaud, to sleep in the streets of Paris at seventeen.

If you remove the physical and sexual experiences many men have made literature out of, you have carved away a great hunk of masterpieces. There is a lot left: James, Balzac, Dickens; the material in these books, perhaps not always in Balzac, is a part of women's lives too or might be "worked up"—legal practices and prison conditions in Dickens, commerce in Balzac, etc.

But the special *vigor* of James, Balzac, Dickens or Racine, the queer, remaining strength to produce masterpiece after masterpiece—that is belittling! The careers of women of prodigious productivity, like George Sand, are marked by a great amount of failure and waste, indicating that though time was spent at the desk perhaps the supreme effort was not regularly made. Who can help but feel that *some* of James's vigor is sturdily rooted in his masculine flesh and that this repeatedly successful creativity is less likely with the "weaker sex" even in the socialist millennium. It is not suggested that muscles write books, but there is a certain sense in which, talent and experience being equal, they may be considered a bit of an advantage. In the end, it is in the matter of experience that women's disadvantage is catastrophic. It is very difficult to know how this may be extraordinarily altered.

Coquettes, mothers, prostitutes and "minor" writers—one sees these faces, defiant or resigned, still standing at the Last Judgment. They are all a little sad, like the Chinese lyric:

> *Why do I heave deep sighs?*
> *It is natural, a matter of course, all*
> *creatures have their laws.*

15 / *The Insulted and Injured:*
Books about Poverty

> "I descend from no name—
> poor from my mother's womb,
> poverty claws me down.
> My father was poor; Horace,
> his father, was the same—
> on my ancestor's tomb,
> God rest their souls! there is
> neither scepter nor crown."
>
> VILLON

Upper Broadway, Riverside Drive, the ulcerated side streets hanging on the edge of the academic plateau, shuddering over the abyss of Harlem and the gully of Amsterdam Avenue. In the 1940's, when I was at Columbia, I used to live in the rooming houses around the University. Those bricky towers in the smoky air had huge, dark apartments inside. Some of them, under sly arrangements violating the rent-control laws, were divided into rooms which were rented singly. Downgraded but still rather collegiate and hopeful, the region was preparing itself with great practicality for the dismal future.

Very little adjustment was necessary for the coming residential exploitation of the Puerto Ricans and the restless Negroes in the next decades. The marigold odor of multiple occupancy, the airless arithmetic of "co-operative facilities," the greasy couches and scarred table tops (furnished) were waiting to receive the bodies of the new tenants, ready to pile them on the top of the bones of the old West Side bourgeoisie whose history and stay in the region have been annihilated, as if by a bomb. Blank brick, dirty mirrors, flaking cherubs on forgotten, undusted cornices. These houses stand now in the menacing scene, bursting with the boredom of the exile, the relentlessly exhausting dissipation of the idle. Sordid dawns and bleary mid-nights; Mayakovsky's "men as crumpled as hospital beds, women as battered as proverbs." The cool, drained look of dark-skinned men lounging on the steps of decrepit Windsor Manor, sodden Carleton House, scandalous Excelsior, leprous Queen's Palace.

Julius Horwitz's novel, *The Inhabitants,* is hopeless as a work of fiction and so should be read for what it is, an important document of our people on Welfare assistance, the West Side rooming houses, the illegitimate children, the drug addicts, the tubercular swains, the squalid kitchens, the rats, roaches, and the eternal, vain search by the state and the mother for the vanished fathers of countless children. "I watched the baby hungrily sucking its milk. The baby would never know happier days." Mothers born on relief have their babies on relief. Nothingness, truly, seems to be the condition of these New York people. They are somehow abandoned by life, and exist without skills or meaning. Blankly they watch the drug addicts rip the telephones off the walls in order to get the nickles and dimes. They are nomads going from one rooming house to another, looking for a toilet that functions. There is a loss of domesticity that the crowding together of several generations cannot conceal. They live in a doom for which none of our concepts has prepared us—the queerness, the uselessness. I think I read recently that before many years have passed it is expected that nearly half of the residents of Manhattan will be living on public assistance. Horwitz gives a vivid picture, through the eyes of a social worker, of this perplexing peculiarity. Is this the world of the destitute as we have been accustomed to think of it? I have stood in front of the houses and imagined every sordid corner. I can feel the crowding, the crying, the dirt, the illness, the hopelessness. There is the soiled, careless white man, a sort of guard, looking after the owner's putrefying property. But out of the houses come the beautiful babies in the Welfare layettes, being pushed along in their new Welfare prams. Infancy is indeed the most prosperous moment in these new lives; they come forth into the world, as if for a confirmation, spotlessly, chastely dressed.

The clothes of the urban indigent are often so nice that only the drunks *look* poor; hot dogs, pizzas from the corner shop, and candy bars prevent hunger. There is a strange lack of urgency, as if all these people had been sentenced to an institution of some kind where food and warmth are provided and where one waits, waits for the father of the baby to turn up, for the lover to telephone, the Welfare check to arrive in the mail. Who would ever have thought that urban poverty would become the nervous fatigue and hopelessness of institution life? For these younger people are not exactly unemployed; for one reason or another—illness, pregnancy, psychological disability—they are tragically unequipped. Our ideas are somehow out of date; they do not really tell us what we want to know about all this. New

York City, with its Bosch-like horrors, its hideous deformities, has this rotten density everywhere. There is some connection between the New York of the "national-market" offices and the old and new slums. It is of the essence that Manhattan should be the "borough of the very poor and the very rich."

In the Sicily of Danilo Dolci's book, *Outlaws,* poverty, hopelessness, hunger, played-out land—classical economic tragedy and suffering—survive, old relics of injustice and indifference. Dolci, formerly an architect, went to Sicily in 1952 to study Greek temple ruins. The misery of the people led him to the decision to dedicate himself to the relief of their condition. He settled in a poverty-stricken fishing village and married a fisherman's widow with five children. The personal decision, the individual act on behalf of mankind, the belief in possibility, the ultimate responsibility: these are still the only relief from guilt and indifference the human soul can offer.

His first book, *Report from Palermo,* dramatized, by the very successful literary method of direct quotation in the language of the people, the plight of the poor at Trappeto. The Sicilian desperation, the extreme conditions of life there have led Dolci to ask for nothing less than a total moral reorganization of society. In *Outlaws,* an account of the people of Partinico, a center of Sicilian banditry, he writes, "The best concerts, films, and plays in the world should be dedicated to the sick of mind and spirit. The least we can do is to see that the highest recompense goes to those with the most unpleasant jobs, those who clean out drains and toilets. . . . A less barbarous society than our own would see to it, at least, that the old, the defenseless, the destitute, and the children, the 'last' of today, were the first to occupy the first-class compartments in the trains and boats and to receive the best treatment in hotels and hospitals, on the most favorable terms or entirely free."

There is an account of Dolci's arrest and prison term which grew out of his project whereby unemployed men began working to rebuild an abandoned road rather than remain in demoralizing idleness. Some of the affidavits offered by fellow writers show an interesting insight into Dolci's character. The novelist Vittorini writes, "I have always distrusted the sort of activity which mixes religion with social reform. As soon as I got to know Danilo, however, all my doubts vanished. And as for his ideas, his plans, and his methods . . . I must admit that I found them eminently suited to conditions in Sicily."

Carlo Levi says of Dolci: "It is this confidence which overflows into the lives of the poor among whom he lives and whose sorrows he has so taken to heart. It is this confidence which has opened their eyes to hope. . . ." As the essence of Dolci's thought Levi chooses the statement: "We are living in a world of men condemned to death by all of us."

The importance of Dolci's literary work comes from his decision to allow the people to speak for themselves, in their own words, without trying to find another form, such as the novel, for their story. When you have actually felt the lives of the bandits of Partinico, at that time Dolci's recommendations have all the urgency of a living need: "If the seven or eight hundred million lire which were found *immediately* for the upkeep of the police force in Partinico alone, had been used *immediately* for building a dam . . . the winter flood waters could have been utilized for irrigating 8,000 hectares and today there would be no banditry and no unemployment."

We are all inclined to undervalue a great rare effort of the sort made by Dolci, and to feel a certan embarrassment about, for instance, Albert Schweitzer. I heard a woman who had met Schweitzer express her dismay that he was more concerned with his *own salvation* than with a disinterested love for the natives!

The Children of Sanchez (autobiography of a Mexican family) by Oscar Lewis. The children of Jesus Sanchez live, along with some seven hundred other souls, in a huge, one-story slum tenement, the Casa Grande, in Mexico City. Not a member of this family has ever known happiness; they cannot succeed or realize their hopes; no matter what drudgery, effort, or inspiration they try to bring to their existence, they will inevitably fail because they were born in poverty. Indeed the four children of Sanchez—Roberto, Manuel, Consuelo, and Marta—are actually sinking into greater deprivation than they were born in. Their efforts are not as effective as those of their father. The children live in a modern state, but they are "marginal," unprotected; they are sophisticated and knowledgeable way beyond their father but it does not yet mean a genuine advantage. The Sanchez children represent in their lives and the drama of their condition something of all the poor young people in all the great cities of the world. In this book about them, the anthropologist, Oscar Lewis, has made something brilliant and of singular significance, a work of such unique concentration and sympathy that one hardly knows how to classify it. It is all, every bit of it except for the introduction, spoken by the members of the Sanchez family. They tell their feelings, their lives, explain their nature, relate their actual existence with all the force and drama and seriousness of a large novel. The stories were taken down by tape-recorder, over a period of years, and under various circumstances. The result is a moving, strange tragedy, not an interview, a questionnaire, or a sociological study.

For a number of years, Dr. Lewis has been making radical literary experiments with his Mexican families, struggling, through them, to tell the story of the poor of the world, to render the actuality beyond statistical truth. And yet he measures his own work by the standard of "scientific" truth, not by the measure of fiction. The huge slum tenement—the neighbors, relatives, lovers, enemies—surrounds the family, enlarging and deepening the personal history so that what one actually has is the story of the condition itself, poverty. Poverty is the fate of this whole world; it is the chief character in this book. The Sanchez family is not of the lowest economic group; the prodigious efforts of the father have given the family a slight, brief lift. The father, a wooden, earnest man, was born in ignorance and destitution in the state of Veracruz. "We always lived in one room, like the one I live in today, just one room." His wife, the mother of the children, dies and Sanchez gradually takes new wives, new mistresses and *their* children, under his harsh but uniquely protective care.

In a world where "marriages" are subject to the most careless cancellation and children regularly abandoned, the sense of personal and family responsibility shown by poor Sanchez has a solemn beauty. By grim labor as a food buyer for La Gloria restaurant and the slow accumulation of further enterprises, he manages to keep an astonishing number of people going. For good reason he is the center of his children's lives, the object of their most intense longings and fears. Roberto says, "Although I haven't been able to show it, I not only love my father, I idolize him. I used to be his pride and joy when I was a kid . . . He still loves me . . .

except that he doesn't show it any more because I don't deserve it." What is so dramatically striking in the story of the Sanchez children is that the same incidents and experiences are described by each one, but with pitifully different interpretations because of pride, natural lack of self-knowledge, and the enormous need of each child to keep the love of his father. The family is hemmed in at every point, confused and desperate, and yet they are powerfully interesting, full of vanity, of piercing if somewhat vague ambitions. They are conscious of hateful disappointments and have to rely, at last, on the mere capacity to endure suffering—a capacity from which little good comes and which cannot give meaning to their lives.

Sexual pride, in both the men and the women, is a strong and often harsh master. The pregnant woman and the illegitimate child; the resentful wife and the unsatisfied husband; the drunken beatings and the bitter mornings; the casual religion and the ultimate hopelessness; the idleness and the dreadful work; the over-crowding and loneliness—alternatives of equal pain, struggles whose unsatisfactory outcome is inevitable. The lives in the Casa Grande tenement are not torpid, but violent and high-pitched. The economy and the nation have no real use for these people, and yet the useless are persons of strongly marked temperaments who must fully experience, day in and day out, the terrible unfolding of their destiny. The story truly inspires pity and terror; we fear to gaze upon these unjust accidents of birth, of nationality, of time.

A previous book by Oscar Lewis, *Five Families*, is just as remarkable and beautiful as *The Children of Sanchez*. In that book, also taken down by tape-recorder and rearranged, the scheme was a single day in the life of five different families in Mexico City, of which the Sanchez family was one. Both *Five Families* and *The Children of Sanchez* are works of literature, even though they are true stories, told by real people. One would ask, certainly, can a work of literature be written by a tape-recorder? It cannot. Lewis's books are both literally true and imaginatively presented. In the end it is his rich spirit, his depth of dedication, his sympathy that lie behind the successful recreation. Lewis's role is that of the great film director who, out of images and scenes, makes a coherent drama, giving form and meaning to the flow of reality. There is repetition in the monologues, but it is the repetition of life and one would not want it diminished. Lewis's hope, as an anthropologist, is that his experiments with the tape-recorder will lead other investigators to the means of understanding and presenting the actual life of the unknown urban and peasant masses. This hope has the charm of modesty, but its fulfillment seems unlikely. It is the directing and recording imagination of Lewis himself that brings to light the dark words of the children of Sanchez, the pitiful summing up of Consuelo. "But though I try to disengage myself, I cannot fail to see what is happening to my family. Oh, God! They are destroying themselves, little by little . . . Now my aunt Guadalupe is like a light going out, a wax candle at the foot of the altar; Marta is but twenty-four years old and looks over thirty . . . Manuel? yes, he will live, but at whose cost? How many times will he test the love of his children by denying them food? It is horrible to think he will survive his own children!"

1961

16 / Disgust and Disenchantment: Some British and American Plays

When Big Daddy in *Cat on a Hot Tin Roof* asks his son, Brick, why he drinks, the answer, teasingly withheld until another drink is offered, finally comes forth as DISGUST, in large type. Big Daddy, exasperated, shouts back in bold type, DISGUST WITH WHAT? Of course, Brick isn't truly suffering from disgust at all, but from a wan, sex-appealy, soaking, local-color *disenchantment*.

When Archie Rice in *The Entertainer* says, "All my life I've been searching for something. I've been searching for a draught Bass you can drink all evening without running off every ten minutes, that you can get drunk on without feeling sick, and all for fourpence," he is expressing a loathing for life that includes himself, his work, his family, England, sex, history, the future. This disgust is so objective, indeed so *reasonable*, given the way Osborne sees his character's plight, that Archie—whiny, sordid, dank hair parted in the middle—has none of that surreptitious emotional appeal with which the stage and films allow their stars to decorate the homeliness of a downbeat role. There is usually a diamond sparkling somewhere about—if only the diamond-brightness of the capped teeth. In the Osborne play, the audience, dismayed by the completeness of Archie's repellent aspect, reminds itself that this coarse, spermy creature is really Laurence Olivier and it is only acting. Thus the humdrum vileness, the familiar measliness may be allowed as "entertainment." Disenchantment will usually deal with the outrageous, the mysterious, the hurt, the elegiac; and disgust will be bare, ordinary, circumstantial. "Thank God, I'm normal!" the priest of disgust sings in *The Entertainer.*

Disenchantment is the current commodity of the American theater. Why can't people really communicate with each other? Why must everything be ugly? Why can't we think of others? And the answers come back, flushed with the tears of the ingenue. Moods of disappointment, dreamy and bitter-sweet, utterly, fiercely private, are the foundation of the plots in Tennessee Williams and William Inge. Yearnings, nostalgic reveries, the blight of childhood, hidden vices —these are the subjects of American theater as Shaw said that clandestine adultery was the subject of the fashionable theater in 1921. Clandestine adultery; how positively solid and beguiling the subject would be after several decades of clandestine frigidity, clandestine impotence, clandestine homosexuality.

Yet the truth is, the commercial and aesthetic truth is, that audiences don't give a damn about childhood, the shock of adolescence, about "communication." Patrons are paying for the sex, not for the dreams, the questions, the moody resolutions. They want to know that the gay, talkative sister in *The Dark at the Top of the Stairs* isn't sleeping with her husband, that the twangy, harness salesman *is* sleeping with an old flame, and doing so with a good deal of self-righteousness because his wife is too sensitive to "communicate" with him. As the curtain goes up on our stage, on a setting plain or baroque in one of the warmer States—near the frontier (Inge) or the plantation (Williams) —domesticity is soon seen to be neurotically pimpled with familiar complexes. Neurotic failure rather than *la nausée* is our theme. Lies, lies, lies—the sympathetic characters moan about life. Failures, omissions, self-delusion—particularly among the women. "Something Unspoken" is the title of one of the single act plays of Tennessee Williams. Ah, something unspoken, once more; neurotic, big-framed old Southern lady-dragon still holding the usual cobweb companion or relation in bondage. The plot turns on an election to high position in the Daughters of the Confederacy: Madame Bolingbroke scheming for the throne.

Still on the stage something must happen and so we get, if not a genuine happening, a sort of revelation that passes for action. An inner light is turned on (Inge specializes in this) and the characters see they have been mistaken, have been playing life wrong, not loving enough, not feeling enough and so on. "Stressing false values" is a favorite revelation among playwrights, even though the recognition of this condition is seldom seen in real life. Tennessee Williams goes in for revelation of another sort. It is not spiritual or moral, but frankly sexual, like a sudden undressing. At the final curtain in a Williams play everyone is running about with his clothes off (Blanche's affairs in *Streetcar Named Desire*, the story of Brick's friend, Skipper, in *Cat on a Hot Tin Roof*, one of Williams's best plays).

Suddenly Last Summer is for the deeply jaded, the hungover. Williams has after all given us everything, and here, desperate at last, he offers up a dish of cannibalism. This is a mistake that profoundly alienates—the awful happening isn't sexual at all; it is a shipwreck not a boudoir tale—and so the plays have to be done Off-Broadway. Cannibalism is the revelation, but the tribal world is peopled with old friends: the tyrant Southern lady again, wheel-chaired, reticuled, fierce-voiced, loquacious, incestuous. She talks and talks, trying to protect the memory of a beloved son against the version of his death which his young cousin, now locked up in a mental hospital, is compulsively repeating. The old dragon's auditor is a young psychiatrist, strangely antiseptic like a piece of surgical gauze; he is very white, white or blond hair, white shoes and socks, light suit, and a white manner. Perhaps this young man is got up to represent the operating table, since he specializes in lobotomies. And the dragon wants the girl lobotomized. Enter mad Ophelia, looking like a member of Martha Graham's troupe, tall, thin, tense, wandering in a Graham maze. The girl tells the story of the son's death, a fate that overtakes him in a place with a very exotic name, sounding like Lope de Vega. The revelation has to do with the son's flesh being eaten by starving young urchins. The white doctor decides not to drill a hole in the girl's head and turns to tell us, the audience, that her story *may* be true. At this point we in the audience can only shout back at the playwright, "Lies, lies, lies!"

The Dark at the Top of the Stairs: Inge likes poetical titles, not sexy ones like *Cat* and *Streetcar*. The revelation in this work is moral or character improving. The young mother has been spoiling her children, trying to keep up with local society. (Stressing false values, not in the Daughters of the Confederacy way, but in the pioneer, Baptist way of Theresa Wright, the star.) Everything is going wrong with this family. The wife is clenching her fists over party dresses, infidelities, and meanwhile her saddle-salesman husband is becoming commercially extinct, like the buffalo, and they may all starve. The young daughter, very sensitive and shy, madly plays classical music on the piano to show her superiority and trueness beneath the shyness. She goes to a dance with a young Jewish boy, Sammy. Sammy kills himself because of a mean snub and daughter *learns*, or has *revealed* to her by life, that she shouldn't have been thinking of her own troubles but of Sammy who was *really* suffering. She sees, as her mother sees when she gets the lecture about the vanishing harness market, that she's been selfish just where she thought she was good. And there it is: regrets, misunderstandings, tearful scenes from the Court of Domestic Relations. Our poor old town, poor Mama, poor Papa; times past in Kansas, old nonsense from the Garden District of New Orleans—and the eternal Delta Dragon reigning forever and ever.

In *The Entertainer*, an empty, squalid music hall performer and his dejected family somehow manage to make a comment upon contemporary life. This dispirited, three-generation assembly, each one obsolescent in his own way, lives in the postwar decline of England and the sheer force of the characters' disgust and despair makes its unbearable and yet indisputable point. In our theater we are so much accustomed to interior history and the private view that the attempt by John Osborne to relate his sordid theatrical scene to the desperate historical present fills the audience with unease and even a kind of suspicion. In psychodrama, Suez and the Welfare State would be considered irrelevant to the "treatment" of the patient. In Osborne's play the thing is exactly the contrary. The disgust would not be altered one bit if the characters were homosexual, incestuous, frigid or whatever. Their peculiar and terrifying obsolescence is not a "revelation" but a fact of history. Their decline is harsh and yet natural, clearly real and not likely to reverse itself. For these reasons *The Entertainer* is one of the most interesting plays since Shaw; for the same reasons it is ugly, and it offends, seriously. Woolcott Gibbs in *The New Yorker:* "extremely distressing but at the same time almost totally meaningless tragedy" and "sheer mindless vulgarity." Brooks Atkinson found this odd, fascinating play "a hollow allegory."

> "Here we are, we're alone in the universe, there's no God,
> it just seems that it all began by something as simple as sun-
> light striking on a piece of rock. And here we are. We've
> only got ourselves."

This is Jean, Archie's daughter by his first wife: existential overtones, politically "angry," on the side of the proles against the middle class, demonstrated against Eden during the Suez Crisis, disgusted with "gloved hand in a gold coach." Jean has a good bit to say, but she is rather dull, much too earnest and thoughtful. (These serious young women wander about plays of every sort, scattering boredom like dandruff on the stage, excused only by the fact that the role may be giving some young female theatrical experience. Indeed the only really interesting girl in the plays of recent years is Maggie in *Cat on a Hot Tin Roof*.)

And Frank, Archie's son, who went to jail as a conscientious objector:

> "Look around you. . . . You'd better start thinking about
> number one, Jeannie, because nobody else is going to do it
> for you. Nobody else is going to do it for you because nobody
> believes in that stuff any more. Oh, they may say they do,
> and may take a few bob out of your pay packet every week
> and stick stamps on your card to prove it, but don't believe
> it—nobody will give you a second look."

The English past is represented by Archie's father, a dignified, dreamy old "entertainer" who is always giving his dignified, dreamy retirement speech.

"I feel sorry for you people. You don't know what it's really like. You haven't lived, most of you. You've never known what is was like, you're all miserable really."

And Archie's tired wife, who drinks too much, and shows those qualities of the lower middle class in England that seem to endure as long as the breath holds out. About the Duchess of Porth, this beaten, boozy wife says, or can *still* say, "I suppose it's a bit silly, but I've always taken an interest in her. Oh, ever since she was quite young. I feel she must be very nice somehow."

These characters are not triumphs of dramatic composition; they are flattened out for the stage like so many pairs of pajamas put through a mangle. They stand for anger, despair, nostalgia, distracted fidelity in the same way that the gin bottle stands for joy, and personal responsibility is represented by urgings to "eat a little something." Still each one has his moment or two and Osborne's dialogue is brisk and vivid enough to carry them along. The whole play is Archie Rice; it is this strange creation of Osborne's and not the meaning to be got from the decline of the music hall art that gives this work its extraordinary character.

So far as the music hall is concerned, Osborne says in his preface to the printed text, "The music hall is dying, and with it, a significant part of England." He dedicates the play to A.C., "who remembers what it was like, and will not forget it; who, I hope, will never let me forget it. . . ." But he has resisted the temptation to use the music hall glamorously or to pad his play with jokes and songs.

The music hall parts are just as grubby, just as unrelieved, just as appalling as the Rice tenement where the rest of the action takes place. "Tatty backcloths," the most antique and hopeless jokes, the scabby, dreary indolence of Archie's act: these brief moments of "entertainment" simply stagger the spirit with their tonelessness, their deathly hoarseness. These tawdry turns, these leers, and above all the terrible, terrible fatigue, the exhausted laughter: no doubt this is the proper requiem for the death of the folk arts.

Archie Rice is the same empty, callous, bored master of ceremonies at home that he is in front of his ROCK 'N ROLL NEW'D LOOK backdrop at the theater. Callousness, not bullying, is the mark of this incredible father and husband—he is as dry as an old lemon rind. "Why should I care? Why should I let it touch me?" he croaks in one of his interludes. Archie's disgust with life, his abysmal carelessness, cover every activity he can conceive of. He chases women, we are told, but romance or even the merest sexual exaltation is impossible for him. "Have you ever had it on a kitchen table? Like a piece of meat on a slab." This utterly nihilistic fornicator likes, dredging up old tin cans from the well of his experience, to generalize too: "Either they're doing it, and they're not enjoying it. Or else they're not doing it and they aren't enjoying it." Archie has a gross and tenacious passion for crude reality. This is not particularly a virtue in his case, nor even a mark of insight; it is a grotesque dividend from his failure to care. He is not a great villain, but a small one given to meaningless love affairs and petty dishonesties. Archie does not assassinate the king, he cheats on his income tax, and while he *fears* nothing he does vaguely *worry* about the ghost of the tax collector who haunts his sleep.

A number of notes are struck in the play; not all of them

are interestingly developed, but a curious excitement comes at every point from the mere attempt to make contemporary noise on the stage. The oily, jangling entertainer threatens; allegory and premonition cling to him like the smell of his costumes, the grease on his hatband.

Endgame by Samuel Beckett is pure disgust, with no other element mixed in. It is a white, covering, freezing snow, nearly unbearable. Utter desolation and hatred of life; ashes, ash cans, blindness, death, slavery, empty tyranny, ghostly giggles, bareness, meanness, starvation. This work has the power to terrify. In sheer pain you go on scene after scene, from nothing to yet another nothing. "Ah the old questions, the old answers, there's nothing like them!" Where one understands the meaning the relief is such that a smile comes involuntarily. "Use your head, can't you, use your head, you're on earth, there's no cure for that!" and

"A flea! Are there still fleas?"
"On me there's one."
"But humanity might start from there all over again! Catch him for the love of God!"

The relief lasts no longer than the batting of an eye. The pitiless misery continues. Is it good or bad art? Complete, merciless, as it is, it has a sort of therapeutic beauty and truth, like the sight of an open grave. It would be presumptuous to say that this misery and disgust are not enough. Indeed it is all too much, the end of the line, and overpowering in the purity of its deathly summations.

1958

17 / Living in Italy:
Reflections on Bernard Berenson

In the rather meek, official narration of the life of Mrs. Jack Gardner, I came across an arresting photograph of Bernard Berenson as a young man, a student at Harvard. Here among the illustrations relating to the subject of the biography (Mr. and Mrs. Gardner with Mr. and Mrs. Zorn in Venice; the Gothic Room at the Gardner Museum, etc.), among the details of ancestry, the accounts of endless journeys and evening parties, of purchases and decisions, courageous endurance and interesting self-indulgence, the passionate, young face of Berenson gazed out serenely, a dreaming animal caught in the dense jungle growth of a rich, lively woman's caprice and accomplishment. This early photograph is a profile, as fine and pleasing as a young girl's; the hair, worn long, curls lightly, falling into layers of waves; there is a perfect, young man's nose, a pure, musing, brown-lashed eye, fortunate long, strong bones of chin and jaw. The collar of the young man's jacket is braided with silk and he looks like an Italian prodigy of the violin, romantically, ideally seen, finely designed, a gifted soul, already suitable to court circles.

We spent the winter of 1950 in Florence and used to go out to see Berenson, as so many had gone before and would go afterward. This unusual man was marvelously vivacious and, in more than one respect, actually inspiring; and yet I would always leave him, somewhat troubled, ungratefully adding and subtracting, unable to come to a decision about him or his life. He was not what I had expected, but I despaired of having an original, fresh or even an honest opinion about him. He was too old, had been viewed and consulted far too much; you had a belated feeling you were seeing the matinée of a play that had been running for eight decades. And even the guests staying at his house approached him with caution, fearing to be taken in by an ancient "tourist attraction." Sometimes one of Berenson's guests would take the night off and come to our apartment in Florence where we would drink too much or talk too much and the guest would return to his host, much too late, defiantly clanging the bell to have the gates of the villa opened. When I thought about Berenson, his young profile of sixty-five years before would come back to my memory, mistily mixing the lost image with the reality of his famous, white-haired, aged elegance, his spare and poetical look, his assurance and his suppressed turbulence. His turbulence and disorderly emotions were not suppressed, I believed, for psychic hygiene so much as for reasons of practicality. In Berenson's beauty there was the refinement, the discipline, the masculinity of a little jockey and some of that profession's mixture of a fiercely driving temperament with the capacity for enjoying a judicious repose. He understood that the proud, small person, believing in art and comfort, must have singular powers and unrelenting watchfulness. Indulgence feminizes; perfection and beauty, without restraint, provoke the unconscious, fatten and soften the will.

At the real beginning of his adult life, Berenson made the profound decision, accepted the necessity for dislocation, and decided to live abroad, in Italy. The fact that Italy was his profession, his art, does not remove the fact of his exile from interest. Ruskin and others pursued the art of Italy without expatriation. It was not a wandering, exiled scholar that Berenson became; he became a sort of foreign prince, a character in a fairy tale with all his properties and drama neatly laid out around him, symbolically ordered. And, indeed, who would dream of severing Berenson and Italy? Where can he be imagined? In Boston? On Fifth Avenue or established on Long Island? He united himself with his residence in the way a nobleman is united with his title and yet, like the nobleman again, it was not altogether convincing as the final existential truth of his life. The depth of the sense of alienation in one so consciously and conscientiously placed is a part of the peculiar affliction and, in another sense, one of the privileges of the voluntary exile.

After the war, Italy came into a multitudinous rediscovery and the old exiles who had been shut off from sight and correspondence for a few years came forth too, as old women with their market baskets appear after a siege. With Berenson, postwar prosperity meant an unexpected sweetening of his public image. His possessions, his worldliness, his aestheticism seemed in a frightened, inflationary world, at the least harmless and, at the best, admirably eternal and shrewd. In the depression decade before the war, his villa, *I Tatti*, with its splendid library, its pictures— its Sassetta and Domenico Veneziano—might have been thought exorbitantly self-centered. In 1950, the first thing I thought about it was that it was not luxuriously beautiful, at least not as such places are abroad. It was not a *paradiso* for an interesting idler, but simply a passable Italian villa, serviceable, comfortable, rather staid, with a good many brownish sofas and draperies. True, it had its garden, its dramatic cypresses and pieces of suitable sculpture, indeed everything graceful and practical that might be expected; still it was most memorable for its solidity, the somewhat Northern substantiality, the thickness of stuffs and things, the reminders of the comfortable Beacon Street standards of Berenson's youth. And the house seemed to ask that the occupants and guests conduct themselves in a discreet and plausible manner, keeping the spirit of reasonable calm and well-polished utility. Politeness, adaptability, the habits of social efficiency were strongly stated if not rigidly demanded; they were the firmness upon which a unique personal history rested. A steady pace, familiar and satisfying, reigned benevolently.

There was no Mediterranean slackness about Berenson, no languor or sunstroke or tropical vegetation. On the receptive, hospitable Italian soil, he built an orderly, conscience-driven life. Heaters glowed in the library; curtains were drawn and brown lamps turned on at dusk. At the fireside you might have been listening to the conversations of a character in Thomas Mann, one of those highly individual scholars in *Doctor Faustus*, with their passionate convictions, their quirks of taste. In the working household there was a noticeable number of non-Italians: a Scotch chauffeur and steady, fair-faced people gave the air of a punctual and neat reliability. Berenson was an intellectual first and, secondly, a person leading a rich and elaborate social life. No doubt, particularly when he was older, some of his habits and needs were suggested by the successful customs of the comfortable, non-intellectual world. He lived with the silky regularity and pleasurable concentration of energies that are at once opulent and sacrificial—the prudence of the sensual. He knew the grace of the steady rounds, the ritual and faithful observance of a kind of liturgical year with its feasts and fastings, its seasonal pilgrimages to Rome and Venice, the stately moves from the winter at Settignano to the summer in the vale of Vallombrosa. He had his morning privacy for work and his afternoon walks. This constancy, rich people seem to think, keeps the bones oiled, provides activity and change without encouraging the hazards or assaults of the unexpected, the wayfarer's disappointments, the explorer's disillusions. Beautiful things, sweet experiences may, like the sudden fluttering of a butterfly on the window pane, appear without warning, but organization, foresight and routine will prevent sleepless nights and throbbing temples. (In his *Sketch for a Self-Portrait*, Berenson cites the fact of heavy drinking in America as one of his reasons for leaving.) No matter, Berenson himself was still the host to all the sufferings of an unusual, gifted nature. There is, it seems, always a hole in the wall where the cold wind can enter.

In Italy, looking about, we remembered Dylan Thomas saying after some complaint of ours about America, "You needn't live in that bloody country, America! You could go somewhere else, you know." The possibility of escape never entirely deserts the greedy dreams of the "self-employed." It flares up and dies down, like malaria; it is a disease arrested, not cured; a question without an answer. The thought that one might himself settle far, far away gives a kind of engrossing sub-plot to one's travels. And the Americans who have made the choice, those colonies with their stoves turned high in the winter, provide the occasional, rushing visitor, resting at the end of the day in his hotel room, with insolent or jealous thoughts.

A man may exile himself for isolation—Santayana in his convent in Rome—for the freedom of solitude, the purity of the release from useless obligations and conventions; or he may exile himself, from America at least, for the freedom of hospitality, the enlargement of possibilities. You may be a hermit or an innkeeper. Berenson's nature destined him to be an innkeeper. Whether he loved humanity or not, he had an enormous appetite for meeting it, being visited by it, for serving it lunch and tea. He seemed helpless before the appeal of a new person, a soul who carried either an accidental or earned distinction. No one was easier to see than Berenson. He could not be called a snob, although his appetite embraced the merely social and the merely rich. When we mailed a letter of introduction to him, he accepted it as a bizarre formality because, of course, he who saw everyone was willing and happy to see yet another. One was never tempted to think it was ennui or triviality that produced this state of addiction; the absorbing inclination seemed to be a simple fear of missing someone, almost as if these countless visitors and travelers had a secret the exile pitifully wished to discover. The expatriate sometimes suffers painfully from the dread of losing touch with the world he has left but towards which he looks back with longings and significant emotions, with guilt and resentment, with all the tart ambivalence of the injured lover. It is, after all, the fickle, abandoned country for which the exile writes his books, for which his possessions are ultimately designated; money and citizenship, nieces and nephews, language and memory—the very skin of life—remain in their old place.

As the years pass, the feelings of loss and uncertainty appear to grow stronger not weaker for those who live abroad. The traveler from home is important, the visitor, the acquaintance passing through bring knowledge, prejudices, fashions that cannot be acquired from the newspapers. A feeling of guilt persists about the very beauty of life abroad, the greater ease, and above all the parasitism of the exile's condition. The dream-like timelessness of Italy is a captivity into which uneasiness creeps. Americans who removed themselves to England were usually seeking manners, civilization, congenial spirits; in Italy the senses were enchanted, brought under the spell of the great sun, the heartbreaking landscape, the sweetness of peasant faces, toiling and enduring, the lemon tree against the wall. It appears that an American cannot become an Italian—property, marriage to the aristocracy, nothing seems to insure assimilation. And the answer must be that Americans want to live in Italy but do not wish to become Italians. Many once wished to become Englishmen and succeeded; foreigners from every land have become Frenchmen of a sort. The Italian exile, with his nostalgic, feudal temperament, is also a person with a wound, not so very different in his feelings from those beachcombers and divorcees in the Caribbean, all who seek to soothe their hurt spirits with the sun, with flowering winters, with white houses opened to the new air and entangled with old vines. Everywhere in Italy, among the American colony, one's envy is cut short time and time again by a sudden feeling of sadness in the air, as of something still alive with the joys of an Italian day and yet somehow faintly withered, languishing. Unhappiness, disappointment support the exile in his choice. Even the endlessly productive Santayana revealed at times his wounds from America and

Harvard. Of his career at Harvard he wrote dryly, that it had been "slow and insecure, made in an atmosphere of mingled favour and distrust." He pretended not to care. He made very little use of Italy; it was a refuge in which he wrote his books, tirelessly.

Was Berenson shady, crooked? Did he make his fortune with the help of false as well as genuine attributions? Whatever the truth, certainly large numbers of his critics and his admirers accepted the charge of profitable dishonesties back in his past. By choosing to use his knowledge for the sale of works of art he brought himself under the suspicion of financial immorality. The "attribution" of venality clung to this famous humanist. Old scandal, dubious gains, lingering doubts, gave a drama and tension to his life; but his work, his books were authentic and he was, himself, a pure creation—that everyone agreed. Berenson lamented that his fame as an art expert "degenerated into a widespread belief that if only I could be approached in the right way I could order this or that American millionaire to pay thousands upon thousands and hundreds of thousands for any daub that I was bribed by the seller to attribute to a great master. Proposals of this nature . . . became a burden; and in the end I was compelled in self-defence to refuse to see people unless I was sure that they brought no 'great masters' with them. Needless to say that every person I would not receive, every owner whose picture I would not ascribe to Raphael or Michelangelo or Giorgione, Titian or Tintoretto . . . turned into an enemy."

Berenson's success, the money he made as a young man, aroused superstitious twitchings among people everywhere, even those who delighted in him as a friend, and certainly among his colleagues. Hadn't life turned out to be too easy for this poor Jewish fine arts scholar from Boston? Was knowledge, honestly used, ever quite so profitable, especially knowledge of art? He had, it was felt, sold himself to the devil by demanding life on his own terms, by asking more than other scholars, by becoming a *padrone* instead of a simple professor. Italian critics were far from hospitable to his ideas and great feuds raged. They did not give over their art to a foreigner without a fight, without accusations and sneers.

Some of the uneasiness felt by the world will inevitably be felt by the man himself. Stubbornness of attitude became a defense for a whole life. A hardening and narrowing, repetition of positions taken long ago, obstinate rejections disguised pain and fear of obsolescence. In Italy, the tremendousness of the past reinforces the spirit in its old assumptions; nothing new seems to be required. It was part of Berenson's idyllic removal that he couldn't like much of the art of his own time. The gods will not grant every gift. He set himself against violence, fragmentation, improvisation, primitivism. He couldn't accept Picasso, Stravinsky, T. S. Eliot, Kafka. He was apprehensive about these productions, irked by the broken forms. He liked Homer, Goethe and Proust, but Faulkner disposed him to fretfulness. He looked upon so many contemporary things with painful distaste and something like hurt feelings. He seemed to see his own essence threatened with devastation. For him, the agile will, the effort to maintain security and preserve courage had been everything. Hesitation, nihilism, abstraction appalled this pulsing ego that had sought to define in his work and personal existence a compact, ennobling, classical example. It was odd that in the lighter arts, in living personalities, he was extremely in-the-know, open to feeling, to humor, to affection, to wild originality.

Pride and conscience urged Berenson to the gritting work of writing. His style was clear and sensible, but literally brought forth in sorrow because he hadn't the luck of ready eloquence, except in conversation. Santayana's contented industry puzzled him. "He loved writing! Preferred it to reading and talking. Imagine such a man!" Still, write Berenson did, and some of the vices and temptations of the literary character were his as much as if he had been living in New York, producing regularly for the art publications. He gave hints of jealousy and of thinking himself under-valued. He was inclined at times to composition on topics that did not deeply engage him, but which he felt necessary to undertake because of wishing to keep in step with subtle changes in taste and emphasis. I once heard another art critic cry out in pain, "That wicked B. B.! He would never have thought of writing a book on Caravaggio if he hadn't known I was doing one!" Berenson noted with chagrin the fee Sir Kenneth Clark was reported to be receiving for his lectures on the nude in the National Gallery in Washington. (The older critic had lived a longer life than most are granted well before the age of plushy lectures, easy endow-ments, fabulous stipends.) His disappointments were only reality, his firm sense of things as they were in life. A deeper truth of his nature was caught in odd moments—I remember seeing him, ancient, regal, stepping along nimbly, like a little gnome king, on the arm of the dancer, Katherine Dunham.

The great age Berenson achieved did not strike one as an accident, a stroke of fine heredity or luck; longevity was an achievement, the same as his books, bought with a good deal of anguish and hard work. His nature, with its prudence, its routine, its rich mixture of work and pleasure, seemed to have been designed for long use. We happened to be paying a call on him in Rome, where he was installed for his yearly state visit like Queen Victoria on her business-like holidays, when the news came that Croce had died. "I should have gone first! The dear man was younger than I!" Berenson said with feeling. Everyone smiled. It was not only that Berenson had lived so long but his wanting to go on living still longer that annoyed certain people. Age was another of his slightly disreputable luxuries.

When he died, at ninety-four, he left, besides his books and the pleasure he had given, a peculiar monument. He left his villa, his library, to Harvard, the home of his lost youth, so that gifted young Americans, interested in art and history, might look out on the Tuscan landscape and be saved from barbarism and provinciality. Berenson seemed to want to leave his daily existence to America, bequeath his setting, his chosen life. Like all his gifts to the world, this too was received with misgivings and hesitation. Did he have enough money to make such a gift? Before she could be accepted the gift must have a dowry, money for her own upkeep, as if she were a bride. "We will all starve! For Harvard!" they used to say in his household. The arrangements were made and the site created by sheer force of personal will and longing would be returned to its source, to be preserved as a little pocket of American intellectual industry, a bit of foreign investment, in the busy Apennines. What endurance and genius had kept alive would go along smoothly, buzzing like the lawn mowers in front of the White House, with the efficient routine of public domesticity. Institutionalized, the villa would soon remind one of those inns taken over by a conquering army. Its occupants will have been chosen and assigned. All those hundreds upon hundreds of guests of the past—the surly writers and old ladies from Boston, the dons, the pansies, the actresses, the historians—won't be coming back to gossip, in a whisper in the halls, about how fortunes were made, to sneak into Florence to get drunk at the Excelsior, and to see the unique Berenson, leading his curious life. At the end, the Pope sent his blessing.